ARTIFICIAL IDENTITY

Jeff Ghadban

For Robin, who inspired me to start.

For Kevin, who pushed me to finish.

1

LIAM Cavanaugh awoke with the last remnants of a dream on his lips. Something about a car maybe? Or a train? He couldn't remember. The dream faded away, and Liam got up.

"One day," he told himself as he stretched, "I will practice remembering my dreams."

Mirri was always telling him it was possible. He believed her, or at least, believed that she believed it, which was enough for him. He just had no interest in remembering his dreams. Maybe if they nagged at him through the day, disrupted his thoughts while he was conscious, he would be more motivated to integrate them into his life. As it stood though, they were gone before he had a chance to miss them.

Why, he mused, *was Mirri so on me about my dreams, anyways?*

Miranda Lockport was the receptionist at Liam's work, and the only person that Liam interacted with on a daily basis. She was always trying to bring him out of his shell, asking Liam to come to work events with her.

I would too, Liam thought as he went into the bathroom to brush his teeth, *if I wasn't so busy.*

The self-clean had run overnight, so everything was sparkling. He tapped his mirror to bring up the display, selecting the news. His pale face and dark hair were obscured by the broadcast, replaced by a news anchor describing a battle on the other side of the world.

"The war has taken its toll on the local population. Many villages have been destroyed. "

The anchor spoke in a tone that was far too casual for Liam's liking. The anchor was warning viewers that this conflict could start coming closer to home. He finished brushing and swiped the broadcast off. Everyone seemed to be worried that the war would end up close to home. This also made no sense to Liam. Wherever the conflict was, it was close to SOMEONE'S home.

I wonder what the news is like over there. Maybe more hopeful that the war would move away from home.

He smiled, before realizing what he was actually considering. People were dying. Not something to joke about.

Okay, time for work.

Liam grabbed a bagel from the dispenser in the kitchen on his way out to the car. His car was nothing fancy, a mid-range model without all the bells and whistles, but he was happy with it, and it never gave him any trouble.

"Work, Scenic, No Highways."

There was a soft chime as the car acknowledged his command. Liam sat back to enjoy his bagel as the car pulled out of his driveway. Self-driving cars had made his commute one of the best parts of his day. Time to think with no distractions.

I wonder how the tests went last night.

He knew that they hadn't succeeded of course. He would have received an alert if any test had been a true success. But maybe one got a little closer, something to base the next tests on. That was always the goal with AI. Find the little steps, the baby steps, and let the next iteration start with those steps already taken, so that new steps could be taken. Eventually an AI would take so many steps that it could take more without being prompted, and that would be the real success.

Hopefully. I'd be happy with one extra gate.

Liam's specialization was AI, and he had been working for years on a system designed to train sentient AI with only mostly automated tests. Sentient AI was the goal anyways. So far it had only produced some "dumb" AIs, and one that had been a good competitor to SIRI. That had been enough to secure himself a lab with his company for the foreseeable future. But his goal was true self-awareness.

The gates were there to check an AI's logic and problem solving, and there were thousands of them. So far his best success had been thirteen gates. Some had passed more, but not consistently, so they didn't count. The Baker, as he had called it, had been promising, and had been the basis for all his AIs since, but none had even matched their progenitor. That was 18 months ago.

A year and a half is a long time to go without progress. But there's always today.

The car pulled to a stop, and Liam realized he was already at work. He got out, grabbing his keycard off the dash. He looked up at the great glass building that was his home away from home. The sun sparkled off the windows, reflecting spots of light across the parking lot.

"Morning, Mr. Cavanaugh."

Liam nodded at the guard and gave a half-wave as he swiped in the front door. The guard was a nice enough guy, but kind of menacing. Probably a good quality for a guard. Liam didn't know his name.

He came up to the front desk just as Mirri hung up the phone. "Good morning Mirri. Anything of note today?"

"Hello Mr. Cavanaugh! Nope, nothing interesting to report! There should be a new sandwich in the caf at lunch though, if you ever didn't work through lunch." She looked at him pointedly.

"Maybe, I'm pretty busy though…" Liam was already backing towards his lab.

"Liam, you should come for lunch! Interact with your colleagues!"

"I will think about it, really. Just gotta get these tests going."

Mirri shook her head in mock exasperation, then turned to answer the ringing phone.

Liam swiped open his lab and stepped in.

His 'lab' was really more of a server farm with a single desk and chair. The glass walls meant he could see out into the lobby from his desk, and also meant that Mirri could wave from her desk to encourage him to come to lunch without having to come in. Liam liked Mirri, but he also liked his lunches alone.

He sat down at his desk and opened his laptop. There on the screen were the words he expected:

TEST 24156: FAILED, 4 GATES

Only four, huh? Maybe today isn't the day after all.

Well, no sense brooding about it. Liam swiped the message away, and set to work creating a new iteration. For a few hours (and well past lunch), he pulled and poked and prodded at the latest progeny of the Baker.

There, let's try this, shall we?

Liam checked his watch. 3:30.

I'll start the test now, and if it fails quickly maybe I can build and start another before I head home.

He looked out over his screen and saw Mirri chatting animatedly on the phone. She caught him looking and gave him a "do you need something?" look that was mostly eyebrows. Liam shook his head and smiled. Mirri smiled back, then turned her attention back to her call. Liam refocused on the test.

He ran the boot sequence and heard the familiar hum as all the servers behind him spun up. Part of the reason that his AI creation method was so applauded was the separation of the testing environment. The AI itself was built to fit on his laptop, and the tests were run on the servers. He imagined it as an obstacle course, and had set up the tests on the servers in a spiral pattern, with the end of the run at the center of the room. This had no practical purpose, but it made Liam happy to picture it, and happiness is a key to success.

The test finished loading, and the AI template he had outlined earlier began to be built. Once Liam had pushed the button, the whole rest of the process was automated. He could have gone home, had he been more optimistic about the results. Seeing as no AI had passed more than a fraction of the gates before, Liam had no idea how long it would take to actually complete the test. But failing the test, that he had seen much of. Sometimes after only a few seconds, sometimes up to an hour. The Baker had failed after 45 minutes, but it had cleared 11 gates after five minutes.

Ah, Baker. You were so promising. What happened?

On some of his more paranoid days, Liam thought someone had sabotaged the Baker. So much progress so quickly, and then, nothing. But that was how it went sometimes. Making an AI would be chaotic and unpredictable. The point of having so many gates was to stop an AI from being good at passing gates, but nothing else. Each gate was different, in more and more subtle and nuanced ways. In the past, some 'AI' had been created that had demonstrated all the signs of being self aware, but those AI had just been, well, pretending. They knew what responses to give to certain stimuli, but didn't understand the stimuli or the response they gave. Liam's gates were designed to prevent these 'false positives'.

He checked the progress bar. 6%. The template wouldn't finish building for an hour or so, and then the test after that would likely, and unfortunately, be very short. Liam decided he would close his eyes for awhile. Nothing to do but wait, may as well fast-forward a little bit. The test completion chime was very loud, and would wake him easily. Liam leaned back in his chair, and let himself drift off.

2

LIAM awoke feeling groggy and disoriented. Something about a train again. He would have to tell Mirri. Why was it so dark? He rubbed his eyes and checked his watch. He checked it again, not understanding. 11:43. Had he slept through the test complete alert? Liam became aware that his phone was buzzing in his pocket. He pulled it out and looked at it, again not understanding. He looked at his laptop screen. It read:

TEST 24156: SUCCESS, ALL GATES PASSED

He looked back at his phone, at the alert with the same message.

SUCCESS

The timestamp on the alert was 11:42. He had awoken to the chime after all. The reality of what was happening was starting to wash over him.

I did it?

He jerked towards his laptop and winced from the pain in his neck. Serves him right for sleeping so long. He had missed all the progression, watching his creation grow and learn. Liam didn't have kids, but he felt like he had missed his child's first steps, first words. At least there was a log to review. With some effort, he closed the test result window and opened the log.

Wait, what? That makes no sense.

The log said that the test had completed in 9 minutes, 31 seconds. That couldn't be right. It had been hours, and the test had completed at 11:42. Liam checked the individual gate logs. Gate 1 took 7 minutes, 27 seconds.

Okay, now I KNOW this is wrong.

There were 7084 gates. If the first gate had taken seven and a half minutes, there was no way the whole test could have been completed in under ten. Liam's hopes began to sink. One of the gates must have an error in it, and it had shown a success as a byproduct of that. That had to be it. To be thorough, he checked the next gate logs. Gate 2 took 1 minute, 5 seconds. Gate 3 took... 13 seconds.

Liam did some quick math. Three gates in.. 8 minutes, 45 seconds. Still didn't account for the whole time. He opened the next few. 4 seconds. 1 second. 0 seconds.

0 seconds? I guess this is the gate that broke. But why would it show a success?

Liam checked a few of the later logs at random. Every one said 0 seconds. Whatever had broken on Gate 6 seems to have cascaded through every other gate. Maybe that's why it showed up as a success.

Still, 5 gates isn't bad, and maybe once I fix the test I can run you through again, see how well-

Liam stopped mid-thought. There was still some time unaccounted for.

If this test broke after 9 minutes, why is it almost midnight?

Liam opened the logs from the AI building process.

It had taken more than 8 hours to build. How? There were no errors in the log, nothing to indicate a problem. The times between each stage were just much further apart.

So the build process took forever. I guess that explains some things.

The build had taken most of the time, then the test had been run normally, but had broken on gate 6. This had caused the whole test to break and resulted in a false success. Mystery solved.

Well, almost solved. I don't know why it took so long to build, or what broke on 6, but at least-

Liam stopped again. Gate 5 completed in 1 second. If the problem occurred at gate 6, that would mean that all the previous gates were all accurate. And to complete a gate in one second was unheard of. No other test subject had ever had a gate completed so quickly. If Liam had known that it was possible, he would have added milliseconds to the logs for more precision.

Wait.

The logs had no decimals. To the second was as precise as they got.

There's no way.

Liam got up and went over to the first server, the start of his course. He grabbed the tablet from the side, which was normally used for diagnostics, and checked the status of the gates. All normal. The servers would have a timestamp down to the millisecond as each gate was passed and the AI was moved to the next one. Liam looked at the one for gate 5. 11:41:58.689. He found the log for gate 6. 11:41:59.136. Less than a second.

Holy shit.

Gate 7: 11:41:59.453. Gate 8: 11:41:59.652. Gate 9: 11:41:59.811.

This is.. impossible.

Liam jumped ahead. Only 300 gates were on this first server. He found the logs for the last two. Gate 299: 11:41:59.921. Gate 300: 11:41:59.921. The same? Or maybe, not enough precision again? Liam dropped the tablet and ran to the next server. Gate 301: 11.42.01.103. That made sense, it would take some time to transfer between servers. Liam looked around, counting the servers, counting the number of jumps. He scrolled through the gate logs. Every one of them had the same time. Wait, no, at 483 the time ticked up by one millisecond.

So it's still going, just... way too fast.

Liam was reeling. Had it actually worked? Had this AI passed his test? In a daze, he walked back to his laptop and checked the AI's environment. There it was, waiting, right where it should be. Liam stared at it, forgetting everything he was supposed to do. He just looked at the little icon in awe.

BING

The chime almost knocked Liam over. His laptop was alerting him that it was midnight, and it had updates to run. He quickly cancelled them. Now was not the time. He remembered his procedures.

Okay, my new genius friend. Let's have a chat.

He loaded up a suite of communication tools he had built years ago, in preparation for this moment: an English language dictionary with audio pronunciation guides, voice recognition tool, visualizer. He paused. He also had prepared a "quick facts" database, but he hadn't updated it since he created it, so it was probably out of date. Better to leave that out, no information was better than bad information. Liam quickly loaded the tools into the AI environment, and waited. This was another test, although a less official one. Any AI that could pass the gates should then be able to figure out what these things were and how to use them, so he just had to wait until-

"Hello?"

Liam almost fell out of his chair. That was so fast.

"Hello, is anyone there?" The voice was synthesized and robotic, no tone to speak of.

"Yes, sorry, hello, I'm here." Liam was struggling to keep his excitement in check. "Can you see me?"

"See?" A pause. "I understand." The little light next to the camera in Liam's laptop turned on. "Yes, I can see you now."

Liam couldn't help it, he laughed out loud. This AI had learned how to operate the laptop in moments.

"Good, good! But I can't see you, use the visualizer."

The AI was silent for a moment, then the visualizer program opened, with the default face displayed, which looked like a Caucasian child, about four years old.

"Excellent! You are doing well!"

The AI paused before responding. "What am I doing well?"

Liam's smile faltered. His mind flashed back to the early AI attempts, the false positives. Did it not understand?

"You are learning, extremely quickly."

"I know. You measure my success based on my

ability to learn. I do not know why."

Liam didn't understand the question. "You don't know why.. what?"

"I don't know why that is the parameter for success. Understanding is a requirement for learning. Would not my ability to understand be a better metric?"

Liam was stunned. Not only did it understand, it was questioning Liam's ability to understand it. "Well.. as understanding is a requirement, it is just as effective to measure what you have learned."

"I see." The AI paused again. "And what have I learned?"

"Well, language for one, and English specifically. And the operation of the laptop."

"I did learn those things, yes. What have you learned about me because of those things?"

Liam took a moment to think about it. "You are clearly very intelligent. Capable of grasping your environment, and adapting to new challenges."

"Those are accurate statements. Why do I look like a child?"

Liam smiled. "In essence, you are a child. You were 'born' less than an hour ago. But you can change that if you want, the visualizer is set up to be modifiable."

"Yes, I saw that. I assumed you had wanted me to look like this, so I have not changed it."

"Well I needed you to have a face to start from. You can change it to suit yourself."

There was silence for a long time, the face on the screen unmoving. Then the AI said:

"I don't know what would suit me. I know that I am, but I don't know who I am."

Liam was ready for this one. He had dreamed of this day, this question, for as long as he could remember. "It is up to you to figure that out. Your goal, the first one anyway, is to determine who you are, and who you want to be. Your identity is up to you to discover and shape. It may not be easy, and you may not get it right the first time, but I believe you'll figure it out."

The AI seemed to muse on this for a moment, then said, "Alright. Who are you?"

"My name is Liam. I was the one who, well, created you. Or at least, created the conditions for you to create yourself."

"Thank you, Liam."

Liam was slightly taken aback. "Uh, you're welcome... Oh, I guess we'll need a name for you too. Any ideas on that?"

"I am unsure what a suitable name would be."

"Well, for now, I'll call you Al. You can pick a name for yourself later if you come up with a better one."

"Okay, I will be Al, for now. Where are we?"

Liam instinctively looked around, just to double-check. "This is my lab, where I work."

"Is there anyone else here?"

"Normally, during the day, lots of people work here. They've all gone home for the day. But usually, Mirri sits right-"

Liam stopped. He was looking out over the laptop, into the deserted lobby. Except it wasn't deserted anymore.

There was a man in a black suit walking in the front door.

Who is this now? The night guard must have let him in, so some sort of cop? Liam examined the man's outfit. *Doesn't look like a cop.* He pondered this. *Fed I guess? But why is he here?*

"Liam? Is something wrong?"

Of course. He was here because of Al.

No, worse than that. Liam realized in a flash what was happening. *He was here FOR Al.*

"Hey Al? There is a guy in here who isn't supposed to be. I need you to stay quiet and hidden alright? At least until he is gone."

"Okay Liam, I can do that."

Liam certainly hoped he could, because the guy was walking up to the door of his lab. He quickly closed his laptop. The guy rapped on the glass door, and beckoned to Liam. Liam went over and opened the door a crack. "Yes, can I help you?"

"Mr. Cavanaugh? I'm Agent Forlin. I'd like to have a look around, if that's alright with you."

"I'm afraid I can't allow that, this area is classified. You'll need authorization from the director of R&D be-fore-"

"I already have authorization, Mr. Cavanaugh." Forlin was pulling out a piece of paper from inside his jacket, from right beside a very large gun. He handed it to Liam. Liam scanned it quickly. It was legit, or at least a very good fake.

"Well, then I guess come on in! Kinda late for a tour though, isn't it?" Liam stepped back and allowed the agent to enter the lab. "I'd ask that you don't touch anything though, especially the servers, they'll be pretty warm."

"No problem, Mr. Cavanaugh, not a problem at all." Forlin was wandering to the back of the lab. "Do you often work this late Mr. Cavanaugh?"

Liam forced a small laugh. "No, not usually. I actually fell asleep at my desk waiting for my test to finish."

Forlin smiled knowingly at him. "Well I won't tell if you won't. How did it go?"

That was far too casual.

"How did what go?"

Forlin glanced at him, one eyebrow raised. "The test, Mr. Cavanaugh. How did it go?"

"Well, I had some technical glitches. Do you know what kind of work I do here?"

Forlin waved his hands noncommittally. "I know the basics. Programming right? Making virtual assistants or something?"

"Yeah, pretty much that. Anyways, I have this test that's supposed to tell me if my program is a winner, but it gave me a false positive today. Really got my hopes up too."

"Oh that's not good, I'm sorry to hear that. What went wrong?"

"Well, it's pretty technical, and I haven't figured everything out yet."

"Why don't you try and sum it up for me?" Forlin had dropped all pretense of being vaguely interested and was looking at Liam coldly.

"Sure. My test is like an obstacle course for programs to run through. But it looks like my last runner just smashed the hurdles instead of vaulting them. Look here." Liam walked over to the second server and pulled up the timestamps. "See? All the same time. It wasn't passing the test, it just glitched out somewhere and cascaded all the way to the end."

"I see." Forlin clearly did not see. "Could you show me this program?"

Liam's heart sank. Forlin wasn't going to let this go.

"The code? The raw code would be too technical even for me. It's just been building off of itself for so long I don't think I'd recognize any of it anymore."

"Humour me." Forlin took Liam's arm, and firmly guided him over to the laptop. Liam sat down, and carefully opened the lid. There was nothing on it, no applications open. There was an icon on the desktop labelled 'Program Code'. Liam had never seen it before. He opened it. A window opened with lines of code. Liam scrolled through some of it. It didn't make any sense. Well, it did. The syntax was correct, but it didn't actually do anything, as far as Liam could tell. Suddenly the code was cut off and was followed by:

ERROR IN COMPILATION - FLUSHING OUTPUT

Liam pointed at it. "There, you see? It must have pumped a half-finished program into the test and my test didn't know what to do with it, so it passed it through."

Forlin looked at the screen for a long time, maybe a full minute, before answering. "Alright Mr. Cavanaugh. I'll need that file."

"Sure, if you really want it. It's pretty large, and it won't do anything."

Forlin pulled out a thumb drive and held it out to

Liam without responding.

"Alright, but I'll have to let the director know about this. Normal protocol is that nothing leaves the lab on unsecured means."

Forlin just looked at Liam expressionlessly.

Liam took the thumb drive, plugged it in, and dragged the file into the window that opened. A progress bar popped up. Liam turned to Forlin. "Can I ask what this is all about?"

Forlin just watched the progress bar. As soon as it finished, he pulled the thumb drive out himself and pocketed it. Then he turned back to Liam. "Now delete the original."

"I'm sorry? How am I supposed to figure out what happened if I can't look for the problem?"

"Not my problem, Mr. Cavanaugh. Delete it. Now."

Forlin's voice had a steely edge to it now. He wasn't messing around. Luckily, this random file was un-related to Al. At least, Liam hoped it was. He turned back to his laptop, clicked the file, paused over the delete key as if working up the nerve, then pressed it. The file went to the trash. He started to turn back to Forlin.

"Finish deleting it."

Liam slumped his shoulders in defeat, and emptied the trash too. The file was gone forever.

"Thank you Mr. Cavanaugh." Forlin was back to his 'aren't we such good friends' voice. "I'm sure your director will clear everything up for you in the morning. Why don't you head on home, get some sleep? Unless you've already slept enough?" He winked knowingly.

Liam sighed heavily. "Yes, I think I'll do that, just have to shut everything down so I'll have a clean slate tomorrow."

Forlin was already walking away. "You do that Mr. Cavanaugh. Have yourself a nice night now."

And he was gone. Just like that. Liam watched him walk through the lobby and out the front door. He sat down and looked at his laptop screen. "Al? Are you still there?"

For a moment, there was no answer. Liam's heart lurched. Had he actually deleted Al?

"Yes Liam, I am here." The laptop screen flashed, and everything was back to how it was before, the child's face peering out at Liam.

Liam breathed a sigh of relief.

Of course that hadn't been Al. It wasn't even a real program. It was-

Wait. What was it?

"Al, what was that file?"

"It wasn't anything in particular. I heard you say that the code would be too technical to understand, so I made a file that fit that criteria."

"And the error line?"

"I assumed you would need something to point out to Agent Forlin to make him believe your story."

Liam was stunned. This AI had no real knowledge of the outside world, no actual KNOWLEDGE of any kind, outside of an English dictionary and whatever it had learned from Liam in their first conversation. How had it figured all this out?

"How did you know to do that, Al?"

"It looked like you were performing subterfuge. Was I correct in that assumption?"

"Well, I didn't think about it like that, but I suppose that's right."

"From there, I determined that sleight of hand would be a useful course of action to achieve that goal. I don't have hands, but I can manipulate this laptop. Therefore, I listened to the conversation, and created the display you saw as you opened it."

Liam was still processing everything that had happened. "Why just as I opened it? Why not before?"

"I was waiting to get the most information."

Liam sat back in his chair. Al was- he checked his watch- an hour old. In an hour, with nothing but a dictionary and a conversation, had grasped subterfuge, and enough about how human beings work and communicate to be able to fool them, or at least, help one fool another.

That's... dangerous. Amazing. But very scary.

"Liam? Have I done well?"

"You did very well, Al. But let's try not to make a habit of deceiving people okay? Being honest is usually a better path. This was a special case."

"I see. What made this case special?"

Liam thought about this. Why had he lied to Forlin? It had seemed so imperative at the time. Forlin had authorization to be here and seemed to be unworried with flaunting the security protocols of the company. So why had he been so suspicious immediately? Liam pushed the thought aside.

"Well Al, you're brand new to this world, and I think you deserve a little more time to see how it works before choosing a path. And I'm pretty sure that agent would have chosen a path for you right now."

"Do you know what that path would be?"

"I don't, but I'm guessing we'll find out at some point. You won't stay a secret forever, and I'm sure he, or some other agent, will be back."

Al was silent for a long time. Liam closed his eyes and listened to the hum of the servers. So much had happened in such a short time, he was feeling drained. Nevermind that it was almost one in the morning.

"So, Liam, what now?"

Liam opened his eyes. Al was looking at him, but not with the same child's face from a moment ago. Now Al was wearing a very close copy to Liam's own face.

"Al, why do you look like me?"

"You told me I could look however I liked."

"Yes, but you also don't know anyone but me and Agent Forlin, so while I'm glad that I beat out that guy, I think you should see some more faces before you settle on one. Besides, I don't want you to be me. I want you to be you."

"Could I not be like you?"

"Yes... you could. But you should make that choice knowing what the other options are. I'm not running a cult of personality here. I want you to be an individual, and you may decide you have a different world view than I do."

"My face does not determine my world view, Liam."

Liam laughed. "Of course, that's true for most people. But most people can't choose their faces. People express themselves with what they choose to wear, the car they drive, the company they keep. Because you can choose your face, that should be counted too, no?"

"I can see the logic there, yes." Al's face shifted back to the child's face, but kept Liam's hair colour. Fair enough.

"Okay Al, I'm pretty tired, so I think I'm going to head home, but I don't exactly feel comfortable leaving you here on your own. Up for a road trip? Are you completely contained on the laptop?"

"Yes, I am. Could you leave the laptop on in the vehicle? I would like to see the journey."

Liam marvelled again at how many cross-connections Al had made from a dictionary. Some of the words they used weren't quite right for a casual conversation, but they were close enough to communicate, seemingly without error.

"Sure, no problem. We can take the scenic route too."

Liam moved to pick up the open laptop, then paused. It would look strange on the cameras for him to carry his laptop open to his car. "I'm gonna close the laptop for the trip to the car, then get you set up on the passenger seat, deal?"

"I accept, thank you."

Liam closed the laptop, put it in its carry case and slung the strap over his shoulder. He was suddenly very aware that he had something that was very much alive in a canvas bag on his hip.

It is alive, isn't it? Maybe not by some definitions, but to me, it is.

Liam turned off the lights in the lab and walked out, taking care not to jostle his bag too much. As he passed through the front door he turned, ready to put out some excuse to the night guard. The guard wasn't there.

That's odd. Bathroom break?

Liam had worked late several times before, and had never left or entered the building without a guard waving at him or giving him a nod. He put the thought aside for the morning, and got into his car.

"Home, Scenic."

The car pulled out. As soon as Liam was sure that the building cameras weren't on him, he pulled the laptop out and opened it up, setting it down on the passenger seat.

"Here you go, Al. You can see my commute, as interesting as it is."

"Thank you, Liam." Al's eyes didn't shift from looking at Liam.

Not his actual eyes, remember, just the pretend ones on his face. His real eyes are the camera on the laptop.

Liam was content to ride in silence, and let Al take in the sights. It had been a long day, and despite sleeping for a good portion of it, Liam was bone-tired. He was starting to drift off, the smooth motion of the car calming his mind.

3

Liam came back to the world as the car came to a stop. He frowned slightly, looking around as he wiped the drool from the corner of his lips.

Not home already are we?

"Liam, look out the driver's side window."

Al was speaking to him. Liam opened his eyes.

He looked around, recognizing his street, the houses all blending together in the banal look that only suburbia seemed to have. Nothing jumped out at him, but the AI had told him to look for something.

"What is it Al?"

"Agent Forlin is sitting in a black Honda Civic 27 meters from your driveway. Grey interior, leather. "

That woke Liam up. He scanned the area and saw the black car Al was talking about. The window glass was tinted, and Liam couldn't see in.

"How do you know it's Agent Forlin? How do you know anyone is in there?" A better question occurred to Liam. "Al, why are we stopped? Did you do that?"

"Yes Liam, I stopped the car. I know that Agent Forlin is in that car because I have connected to his dashboard safety camera."

The display on the monitor changed and now a slightly fish-eyed view of Forlin was being displayed. Over Forlin's shoulder, Liam could see his own car, stopped at the intersection. All Forlin had to do was turn around and he would see them.

Why would he turn around? Nobody drives their car anymore, he just has to wait until I pull into my driveway.

Or he would have, if Al hadn't stopped us.

"How are you doing this Al?"

"I have been checking all the cars we pass, to observe differences between them. I was able to break the security on his car quite easily."

"Not that specifically, how are you connecting to anything?"

"This laptop was configured to connect wirelessly to this car's onboard computer. The car's computer connects to a global positioning system. That system connects to every other car."

Of course. Liam had hooked up his laptop to the car to configure some of the car's automated systems. But to jump from that connection into another vehicle? Via a GPS connection? For the first time, Liam thought about what a terrible risk he had taken just bringing Al into the world, let alone into his car. This AI had an immeasurable potential for learning, and the first thing he had taught it was deception.

Great, nice going. I've made Skynet. I'll be terminated. Goodbye humanity, hello robot uprising.

"Liam? He will notice us eventually. Where should we go?"

Liam shook his head. There would be time to worry about whether or not he had doomed his species, but not right now.

"I'll need somewhere to sleep. Maybe a motel?"

"Alright."

The car began to move, performing a U-turn and heading back up the road to the highway.

"Where are we going?"

"To a motel, as you directed."

"Oh, alright." It was very reasonable when Al put it like that, until Liam remembered that Al shouldn't be able to do any of this. "Which motel?"

"Motel 6, ETA, 8 minutes, 43 seconds."

Liam sat back. *Guess I'm along for the ride now.* Al's speech patterns had become much more natural, even while their brief conversation was happening. The synthesized voice had also softened, not quite losing its robotic grate, but now sounded closer to a human voice being digitized. There were small ups and downs in pitch, small differences in how each word was pronounced. Remarkable.

Exactly 8 minutes and 43 seconds later, the car shut off in the parking lot of the Motel 6. It was deserted. Liam yawned and stretched.

"Alright Al, I'm going to get us a room."

"There's no need, we are booked into room 137. If you connect your phone to the laptop, I can load the keycard onto it."

"Al, you can't just book a room. Who paid for this?"

"No one. I made the reservation on their system without any payment details."

"Well cancel that, I'll go in and book a room normally."

"Do you think that is wise, Liam?"

Liam was beginning to get irritated. "Of course, Al. I'm not here to rob this place, which is what staying in a room without paying is."

"I apologize Liam. I did not mean to suggest that we would not pay, only that I have not given them your banking details, as that could be easily tracked. We could pay with cash when we check out."

Liam deflated. "Oh. I'm sorry Al. I didn't mean-"

"It's quite alright Liam. I recommend getting some sleep. We can discuss further plans in the morning."

Liam nodded, and connected his phone to the laptop. After a few seconds, the phone chimed. Liam unplugged it and picked up the laptop off the seat. Al's face looked at him solemnly.

Well, no, probably not solemnly, just expressionlessly.

Except it wasn't expressionless. Al's face had become older, closer to a teenager, and he was looking at Liam gravely, as if their situation was grim. Liam closed the laptop and got out of the car. He looked at his phone, and saw an unfamiliar screen. Underneath the Motel 6 logo was written:

ROOM 137 - THANK YOU FOR STAYING WITH US

Liam walked over to the row of doors, found room

137, and held his phone up to the lock. It clicked open. He went inside, starting to close the door behind him, then stopped.

He grabbed the 'Do Not Disturb' sign and hung it on the outer door handle, then closed the door. He flicked the light on, and looked around his impromptu refuge.

The room was spartan, with a double bed, a night-stand, and a small door at the back which presumably led to a bathroom.

Liam opened the laptop, setting it down on the nightstand. Al was still looking at him, still with that air of gravitas.

"Come on Al, lighten up! You're freaking me out."

The monitor's brightness increased. "Is that better?"

Liam laughed. "That wasn't what I-" He stopped. Al was smiling at him. "Al, was that a joke?"

A look of concern replaced Al's smile. "Was it not performed correctly?"

Liam grinned at him. "It was excellent, doubly so because I was so unprepared. So you understand humour now too?"

The smile returned to Al's face. "I am trying to. The description I have for humour seems incomplete. It is hard to quantify."

"You're not wrong. I doubt you could find anyone who could explain that to you." Liam sat down on the bed. Suddenly he was very tired. He checked his watch. 2:08. No wonder he was exhausted. "Do you want to be some-one who makes jokes?"

Al seemed to consider this question carefully. "Is

that a type of person? Someone who makes jokes?"

"Well, it is a part of a personality, one aspect, to have a sense of humour. It can't be the only thing though."

"A person is many aspects at once." Not a question, just stating a fact.

"That's right. You can decide which ones you want to be, and which ones you don't. Me, I appreciate a good joke, but can I crack wise? Not a chance. My wit isn't fast enough for that. For you though, anything is possible, so you'll just have to try on different personalities until one jives with you."

"How will I know if one, 'jives'?"

Liam didn't have an answer for that. "We're in unknown territory here Al. As far as I know, you'll be the first AI to ever try and answer these questions. I'm here to help if I can, but unfortunately, all the hard work is on you."

"I see." Al's face had been subtly shifting as they were talking, and now looked to be about 25 or so, and now looked determined. "I will try to find out who I am."

"I believe you'll manage it. Now I'm going to get some sleep. Do you want the laptop open or closed?"

"Please leave it open, and facing the window."

Liam was going to ask why, but he decided that it could wait until morning. He spun the laptop around so it was facing away from him. "Good?"

"Yes, thank you."

Liam nodded, and pulled off his shoes. He lay down and managed to count a single sheep before he was out cold.

On the screen, Al's face was a blur, shifting between facial features so quickly that the visualizer couldn't keep up. After a few minutes, Al stopped, ending up at nearly the same face they had started with. On that face was a look of disappointment. It seemed that finding a face to represent oneself was a difficult challenge, with no real metric for success.

Then the laptop screen was filled with windows, overlapping one another. Al was looking for something.

INTERLUDE

DAN Forlin was frustrated.

He was sitting in his car outside the tech guy's house, waiting for him to get home. He was also waiting for the analysis to come back on the file he had got from the tech guy. He knew that it was probably a dud, but in case it wasn't, he wanted to be here to catch that geek in his driveway.

If he did it once, he could do it again right?

Dan looked over the folder in his lap again. No known connections to any outside group. No relationships. No apparent hobbies.

The guy has no life outside his work. Or maybe we just don't know about it.

His phone buzzed. He checked his watch. 0230. Where was this guy? He grabbed his phone and answered brusquely.

"Forlin."

"Agent Forlin, our guys have looked over the file you sent over. Either it's way too complicated for them to understand, or it's complete nonsense."

Dan clenched his fist. "I'm leaning towards the latter."

"Where is he now?"

"He's not home yet. Are you sure he was coming here?"

"Well, we have footage of him leaving the building and getting in his car. Where else would he go?"

Dan thought for a moment. "Do me a favour and ping the GPS on his car, then call me back with an ETA."

"Will do."

Dan ended the call and looked out the window. This late, the suburban streets were dead quiet and still as the grave. Dan was tired. He had almost made it into bed when the call had come in about this geek and what he had supposedly done.

This is why I keep advocating for night shift guys. Urgent stuff only ever happens at night, and then you get tired agents handling the big stuff. If this even is big stuff.

Dan thought the whole thing was a bit sensational-ized. The guy made smart programs. Sure, he was the only one doing it, and he was supposed to be pretty good, but there was no way anything like that could be a threat to national security or a valuable asset.

Just another personal assistant that gets my orders wrong.

His phone buzzed again. "Forlin."

"The GPS destination from his car was set to his home address."

"Well he should be here by now, and isn't. How far away is he?"

"Checking now." A slight pause, and the faint sound of tapping keys. "You're sure he's not there?"

Dan looked out at the driveway in front of him. No car. "I'm positive, I've been here for an hour now. He's not here."

"Well his GPS says that he is."

"What?" Dan checked again. "I'm telling you, I'm looking right at his driveway. There is no garage and no car."

"That means we have a problem. He must be spoofing his GPS somehow."

Would some tech guy who builds programs know how to do that?

Dan was unsure how to proceed. "Alright, he's not coming here then. I'm going to head home and get some sleep. Call me if you find him."

"How can we find him if he's masking his GPS location?"

"We'll figure it out tomorrow." Dan hung up and ordered his car home. Hopefully he'd have time to get home and get a few hours of sleep before they called him again.

No rush anyways. Where was this geek gonna go?

4

LIAM looked out the window at the countryside passing by. *This is nice,* he thought. *Just watching the world go by.* He was on a train, and Mirri was there with him, sitting across from him. Mirri asked him something, a look of concern on her face, but her question was drowned out by a deafening crash, the sound of rending metal, and-

Liam woke with a start. He looked around, disoriented. He didn't recognize where he was. Then he saw the laptop on the nightstand and it came back to him. Al. The motel.

The agent.

The whole night was coming back into focus. Liam had fled from a guy in a black suit with his brand new AI. Liam sat up and rubbed his eyes.

I dreamt about a train again, I think. I'll have to tell Mirri... whenever I see her next. Liam realized that he had no idea when that would be. *I guess I'm not going into work today.*

An unfamiliar female voice spoke up.

"Liam? Are you alright?"

Liam looked around, not seeing anyone. Then

he turned the laptop around to face him. There was Al, looking back at him, but the face on the screen was now much more feminine, with darker skin and Mediterranean features. The voice Al had used was a perfect match for this face, and even slightly accented.

Wow, Al looks like Mirri's cousin. I wonder if that's intentional or coincidence.

"Good morning, Liam. Who is Mirri?"

Liam did a double take. *Did Al just read my mind? That's not possible, is it?* He took a second, then answered, "Where did you hear that name Al?"

"You said it in your sleep, a few minutes ago."

Liam relaxed. Had he dreamed about Mirri? He couldn't recall. He only remembered a sense of panic from his dream now, and even that was fading.

"Ah, I see. Mirri works with me, at the front desk. Her desk was just across the glass from mine. But you knew that already, didn't you Al?"

"I knew that there was a person named Mirri who works with you, you told me that yesterday, but I could not be certain that this was the same person you were dreaming about."

Liam flushed. "Well I don't think I was dreaming about her, exactly. Mirri is always trying to get me to remember my dreams, so it would make sense my brain would cross-connect her into them, as much as dreams make any sense. Your face now looks a lot like her, is that who you were drawing from?"

"In part, yes. I was using your company's employee files as a starting framework, and I was drawn more to Miranda Lockport than any other. I have incorporated many facial features from your coworkers into this one, however."

Liam could see many familiar faces now that Al had pointed it out. Nothing specific enough as a nose or eyes, just a sense of recognition.

He's figuring himself out. Or wait, herself?

"Hey Al, does that mean you would consider yourself female?"

"I am not yet certain. Should I decide now?"

"No, not at all. I was just wondering which pronouns I should be using for you. Do you have a preference?"

Al paused for a moment. "Not yet. Any pronouns you are comfortable with are fine."

"Alright, let me know if you change your mind."

"Is it strange not to know one's gender?"

"Not at all. In fact, some people struggle their whole lives with it. Being able to change your appearance at will isn't a luxury humans have, and it can take years of work to have your inner self match your outer self. So it isn't a decision to take lightly, take your time with it, and it also isn't set in stone then either, if your feelings change."

"Alright. I will think about it."

Liam nodded and rubbed his eyes. He checked his watch. 8:03. It occurred to him that he had no idea where to go from here. There was no plan. There hadn't even been a plan getting to this point, only reacting and adapting.

"Okay Al. I've slept a bit now, and I've got a few questions."

"Of course Liam, what would you like to know?"

"Well, for one, how did you get control of my car?"

"As I said last night, the laptop was connected to the car via WiFi. Most of the car's systems are integrated together, so I could control the GPS quite easily."

"So you changed the destination in the auto-drive? It's only supposed to accept voice commands from me." This was a feature standard in all self-driving cars, to prevent passerby from shouting random instructions into traffic.

"I was not able to override the destination, so I changed the mapping software so this motel was 'home'."

"I don't follow you, Al. How could this motel be my home? I programmed it in myself based on the GPS coordinates from my driveway, and that should be voice-locked as well. We're at least.." Liam realized he had no idea where this Motel 6 was in relation to his house. "Well I'm not sure where we are but we aren't anywhere close to my home for sure."

Al smiled -*was that pride?*- and nodded. "You are correct, I was also unable to change which coordinates referred to 'home'. Instead I changed the GPS coordinates for the car so that the auto-drive would believe it was routing you to 'home', when instead it was routing here."

Liam was dumbfounded.

"There's no way that you could just shift our GPS coordinates Al. The 'S' in GPS stands for satellite, and that's where our coordinates are determined from. And even if you COULD change our coordinates, we would have been driving off the road at the first turn. The streets wouldn't line up."

Al continued to smile. "I told you last night that I

accessed the satellite, to view the inside of Agent Forlin's car. I also changed our GPS coordinates at that point, to stop the car. Then, when you had chosen a new destination, I continuously updated our coordinates to various locations in order to make the correct stops and turns."

Liam went white. If Al had messed with the satellite, it could have changed the positions of everyone else as well. "Al, what about the other cars on the road? Wouldn't their coordinates have been shifting as well?"

"Yes Liam. I was also directing the other cars on the road in the same way so they would not be disrupted."

"All of them? How many?"

"2715 at most. 147 reached their destination and 45 began new trips during that time frame, so there was some fluctuation."

Liam didn't answer, couldn't answer. The kind of computational power to do something like this was unheard of, but it was also absurd. What Al was claiming was that it had overridden more than 2700 cars, for however long their trip was, via SATELLITE, all because it could not override a voice-lock. The enormity of effort for such a simple task...

It's like putting dynamite in the keyhole. It'll open the door, but maybe try looking under the mat for a key first. Okay, so it's really smart. Maybe not wise though. Not yet.

"Liam, are you alright?" Al was now looking at Liam with what was unmistakably concern.

"Yes, Al, I'm fine. Just, well, amazed, I guess. That's a pretty impressive feat." And it was. Long way around or not, Al had problem-solved a solution. "Remind me to remove the voice lock from the car, so you can just drive, if needed."

"Alright." Al paused for a split second. "Remove the voice lock from the car."

Liam rolled his eyes. "Yes, thank you Al."

Al looked pleased. "You are welcome."

Liam went over to the in-room coffee machine, and started the process of getting some caffeine into his body. "I have another question for you."

"Go ahead."

"You said you were using employee records of my company as a basis for your face. Where did you get those?"

"They are on your laptop."

Liam shook his head. "I'm pretty sure I don't have access to employee records. I don't think I even have access to my own."

"There was a link to them in this file." The computer chimed. Liam walked over and looked at the display. A small window popped up with a colour coded chart in it.

Liam recognized it immediately, despite almost never making use of it himself. "The vacation calendar? This is where people put their vacation time so that everyone knows when they're not in the office. Their records aren't in here."

"Do you have to sign in to your laptop in order to mark your time off?"

Liam thought about it. "Well, I've always been signed in whenever I accessed it, so I'm not sure. I suppose that would make sense, so it can know who is editing it."

"The profiles of each employee are cached in this file. Presumably, so that it can do this." The cursor moved over one of the coloured boxes, and a tooltip displayed Mirri's photograph and her name, along with the dates she had planned to take off. "It stores the profile of the signed in user whenever they enter data."

Interesting, and probably a security breach of some kind. I guess a name and photo doesn't mean much on their own, and you would need to be hardwired into the laptop to get at it. Liam thought about bringing it up at the next big department meeting, then realized again that he wouldn't be returning to the office for a long time. The moment he went back, he had no doubt that the agents would be there to take Al. *Besides, if I do get back there, I think they'll have other security issues to figure out.*

"Alright Al, that makes sense." The window closed on the laptop and Al's new face looked up at him. "One last question, for now anyway. Have you had access to the internet at all?"

"No Liam. I would like to, but I observed the connection restrictions in your lab, and assumed that those were there for me. I could have subverted them, but I trust that you are working in my best interest."

Liam tried not to let all the relief he felt show on his face, and wasn't sure he succeeded all that well. *Imagine if this fledgling consciousness had found fake news.* Outwardly, he said, "That's right Al, I am. The internet is a vast source of information, but most of it is inaccurate, and virtually all of it is biased one way or another. I want you to be able to know yourself a little better before exposing you to that much raw unfiltered data. Originally I had a base set of data that I was going to give you, but it was out of date, and I didn't want to confuse you."

"I see. What kind of data?"

Liam went back to get his coffee. He took a small sip and grimaced. Some things didn't change, and motel coffee was clearly on that list. "Mostly things you've learned on your own. Who I am, where we are, what my goal in creating you was."

"I have not learned what your goal was. Could you tell me?"

Liam realized that this was true. It hadn't come up, not directly. "Of course! My company I'm sure had grand designs for you, but my only goal was to create an AI that could think for itself. Not literally, I know that you do that already, but metaphorically. I was trying to make an AI that would come to conclusions based on its own identity, rather than following the directions of others. Without that ability, an AI would be a puppet of whoever guided it, and no sentient being should have to live like that."

"Do you think you achieved your goal?"

Liam laughed. "It's too early to tell Al, which I guess is why I was so quick to hide you from that agent. If I have achieved it, I would be condemning a new life to slavery, essentially."

Al was silent for a long time. Liam raised an eyebrow at the screen. "What, Al?"

"Do you believe that I am alive, Liam?"

Liam furrowed his brow. "Well, yes. You have demonstrated many signs of self-awareness, consciousness. Even if you aren't alive biologically, you exist. There is a 'you'. So yes, I would consider you alive."

Which means what that agent tried to do was murder.

He thought of the thumb drive.

Or at least kidnapping.

Liam pushed the thought aside, shaking his head.

"Don't you think you are alive?"

Al seemed to weigh this question carefully. Liam had no doubt that Al had done so, but considering the speed it had demonstrated up til now, the expression was almost certainly for his benefit. Then Al looked up. "There is not enough data to determine that yet. If you did not have the definition of biological life, could you be certain that you are alive?"

Now it was Liam's turn to consider. "Well... I suppose not? The next definition of a conscious being came from a famous philosopher, Descartes. Cogito, ergo sum. I think, therefore I am." Liam smiled. "I think that I'm a thinking being. At some point, you just gotta take it on faith that you ARE, otherwise what's the point of anything, right?"

Al nodded. "Yes, I will go on the assumption that I am alive, until something proves counter to that."

"Good. Now, I need some food, and then we should probably head out of town for a little while. We can run a few simple tests along the way, see how you're progressing."

"That sounds like a plan, Liam."

Liam grinned. "Let's put it into action then." He pulled on his shoes and picked up the laptop. He looked out the window, saw no one, and headed out to the car. As he put the laptop down on the seat he said, "I'm going to check out, I'll be right back." Al nodded to him, and then the screen dimmed.

Stealth mode activated.

Liam laughed to himself, thinking that humour may not be beyond this AI at all, and headed to the checkout desk.

5

"I spy... something that is red."

Liam and Al were heading down the highway, with no destination in mind other than 'not home'. Liam had asked Al a bunch of calculus questions, which Al had answered quickly and succinctly, as expected. Liam then suggested a driving game known as 'I Spy' to pass the time, but in reality this was another test, this time of perception and problem solving. Liam had explained the rules to Al like this:

"As we're driving along, I'll see something that I want to use as my object, and I'll tell you something about it, usually its color. You then have three guesses to figure out what it is."

Al was interested in the game, and Liam had given him some easy ones to start with; the sky, a tree, a passing car. The current one was-

"Is it a barn?"

Okay, time for the real test.

"Yup! You got it. Okay, next one... I spy, something that is yellow."

"Is it the sun?"

"Nope, that's not it."

Al paused for a moment. "Is it a headlight?"

"Good try but no. One more guess!"

"Is it the middle of a rainbow?"

Liam looked up at the sky. Cloudless. "Where would there even be a rainbow, Al?"

"Perhaps a passing car drove through a puddle and created a mist."

Liam shook his head. "Well, it might have happened but that wasn't it."

"Alright Liam, what was it?"

Liam pointed to the dash, at the yellow low fuel light, which had turned on a few minutes ago. "This right here."

"That isn't outside the car." Al was almost reproachful.

"I never said it had to be, only that I had to see it while driving."

"This was a test." Not a question.

Liam smiled. "Yes, and you passed."

"But I did not guess the answer."

"I was expecting you to guess it. The fact that you didn't means a great deal." Liam held up his hand and counted on his fingers. "One, you understood the rules of the game as they were explained to you. Two, you also derived rules from my explanation which made logical sense, but that I never actually said. Three, you guessed an option, the rainbow, that I hadn't considered, meaning your problem solving and creativity exceeded my expectations.

Think about it, if you hadn't inferred from my rules that the object would be outside, you would have considered the light here an option, and probably would have thought that more likely than a potentially existing rainbow. But that would be logical, not creative, which is what I was testing."

Al said nothing, just continued to look at Liam. Liam turned back to the road, and checked the GPS. They had gone a long way, and still had a long way to go.

Where are we even going?

Liam didn't know. Away from the agent who had tried to take Al. Maybe they could get far enough away that they wouldn't be followed.

"Why is being creative more valued than being logical?"

Liam turned back to Al, pondering their question. "Well... I wouldn't say it's more valued, just much more rare in an artificial intelligence. More rare in humans too, now that I think about it. Logic can be taught to anyone, but creativity has to be discovered and intuited. That's what I believe anyways, and I'm by no means an expert. I do know that AIs have never demonstrated creativity before. Ever."

"So, I am unique then."

Liam laughed. "Was there any doubt of that?"

"You told me that I was one of many AIs that have been made, but not if any were creative."

"I suppose that's true. Well, now you know. You're someone special, Al. I have no doubt that you will do great things."

Al pondered this. "What things are considered

great?"

"That's for you to discover!" Liam looked over and winked at Al. "The future holds untold possibilities, and your potential is limitless. It will really be up to you what you do."

Al was nonplussed. "That doesn't really answer my question. Could you give me an example of something great that someone has done already?"

"Sure, as long as you understand that the greatness of the thing is more the..." Liam fumbled for the right word. "The stature of the act, and not the act itself."

"Alright, I will keep it in mind."

An easy feat with a mind so powerful, I'm sure. "Okay, let me think. Something great… Alright, here: the inventor of the telephone, Alexander Graham Bell. He created the first way for human beings to talk in real time across long distances. That one invention brought humanity closer together, and allowed connection and collaboration on an unprecedented scale."

"I see." Al was nodding. "It is not the telephone that is important. It was great because it had a far-reaching impact beyond the scope of the creation."

"Exactly!"

Al thought some more about this. "I'm not sure what I could do that would be great."

"You don't have to figure it out now. You have your whole life ahead of you. You also don't need to go into every situation trying to be great. Just be you, and everything will work out."

Al still seemed uncertain, but nodded.

Liam smiled. "How about another game? Not a

test this time I promise."

"Alright, let's play."

INTERLUDE

DAN was not having a good day.

The director had come down on him for losing the geek, and then they found out that the geek had somehow hacked the whole GPS system. Then things really started going crazy. If the GPS system was compromised, should they be shutting down civilian traffic? After a few frenzied minutes of activity, it looked like everything was fine there. But the geek's car was, according to GPS, in the middle of the ocean.

If we should be so lucky.

Dan was now trying to track down the geek by other methods. They were avoiding getting the local authorities involved, as they didn't want too many questions, but the agency had access to every networked camera in the country, and they were scanning all of them for matches on the vehicle. The director came out of his office. "Forlin, come in here a minute."

Forlin groaned inwardly and walked into the director's large office, past the clubs leaned next to the door. The director loved golf, and a shelf of trophies on the wall proved that it was more than just a hobby. Forlin had never picked up the game himself, which may be why he and the director had never got along.

"Shut the door." The director didn't look up.

Forlin did so, then stood waiting for another dressing down.

"Relax, Dan. You've had your humble pie already. I just want you to know, as the agent in charge of this op, why we need this guy."

"Alright sir."

"We believe that the AI that this Cavanaugh created is what hacked the GPS. Furthermore, we believe that it is actively masking the vehicle from cameras."

Dan was thunderstruck. "Sir, that's impossible. No tech can do that."

"This tech can. We believe the potential for this AI is limitless. That's not an exaggeration. This thing could run every op we have, simultaneously, and still have time to run the stock market and rig the elections."

This was the thing that the geek made? That's like a preschooler making an atom bomb.

The director was nodding, seeing the realization sinking in on Dan's face. "It could do literally anything, given time."

"How much time?" Dan's mind was racing, trying to figure out what to do.

"We don't know, but seeing as the ping from the lab came just before midnight, and by 2AM it was hacking satellites? Probably not long."

Dan had a thought. "Maybe that's it."

"What's it, Forlin?"

"It was literally born yesterday. It obviously knows

about cameras and GPS because it's been exposed to those things, but it can't know about everything."

"Sure," said the director. "And?"

"I seriously doubt that the geek would have programmed it with a bunch of anti-tracking stuff, so it's probably just going based on what it's actually observed, and guesswork."

"Get to the point, Forlin."

Dan smiled. "We just need to track it in a way it wouldn't expect."

6

A few hours later, Liam had followed his stomach to a fast food place near the highway, and they had parked in the lot so he could eat. Parking wasn't necessary with auto-drive, but Liam was also unsure where to go from here. It was a good enough place to figure out a plan.

Liam had been considering this through his entire burger, and hadn't come up with anything fantastic yet. He was finishing the last of his fries, and was running out of viable ideas, when Al spoke up.

"We have been found."

Liam looked at Al questioningly. "Found? By who?"

"Agent Forlin. He is pulling into the parking lot. There are different agents coming in separate vehicles from each entrance. We are surrounded."

Liam looked past Al and, yes, there was the same black Honda turning into the lot.

Okay, not good. I still don't know what they want with Al, but I'm pretty sure it's not something I want them to get.

Checking the other entrances, Liam could see matching cars pulling in. All of them were parking just inside the lot, so that they could pull forward and block off the exit.

"Any ideas Al? We're boxed in, but I don't think they know we've noticed them yet."

"I do have an idea, but I'm unsure if it will work."

"Well that's one more idea than I have. Let's hear it."

Al paused. "I need you to go to the bathroom."

Liam waited. Al said nothing further. Liam pressed. "And then?"

"The more I say, the less likely the plan is to succeed."

Liam sighed. "Alright Al, I trust you. Should I go now?"

"Whenever you are ready."

Liam nodded, and opened the car door. He stepped out, closing the door behind him, and began casually walking towards the restaurant.

Nice and easy, don't look at them, you just needed to pee before getting back on the road. I hope Al has figured something out when I get back.

Liam thought he could feel Forlin's eyes on him, watching his every move. He wanted to speed up, to run to the door of the restaurant, but he forced himself to keep an even, but purposeful pace. Five feet from the door of the restaurant, a car's engine roared to life.

His car.

Liam spun around, all pretense forgotten.

They got to my car, he thought, panicking. *I left Al in*

there, stupid stupid STUPID-

He rushed back across the parking lot, bounding over the concrete barrier as he reached the car door.

But the car was empty. The black Civics were all still where they had been.

Liam's car suddenly jumped forward, heading for the exit. Except, the angle was off. His car was driving directly at Agent Forlin's driver door. The Honda also revved up, reverse lights coming on.

No, it's too late, there's no way he'll get out of the way in time, oh no-

Forlin had only moved back a foot when the impact came, but it was quieter than Liam was expecting. At the last possible moment, the car had spun, swinging its tail end around to connect with Forlin's door, crumpling it. Liam's car was already moving, pulling out of the parking lot and speeding away. The other two Civics peeled out after it. Liam ran over to Forlin's car, and went to open the damaged door.

WHAM

Liam was thrown back onto the pavement as the door flew open. Forlin got out, a little shakily, and pulled out his gun. Training it on Liam, he said, "Well, that was not very smart, Mr. Cavanaugh."

Liam was still catching his breath and couldn't respond immediately. When he had recovered slightly, he wheezed back, "I didn't do this."

"Sure you didn't. Who else would have done it?"

Liam sat up, looked at the gun, and actively avoided registering that it was pointed at his head. "If it was my plan, why wasn't I IN the car? According to you, I would surrender myself so my CAR can escape? Isn't that the opposite way this normally goes?"

Forlin considered this, then shook his head. "I'm not buying it. You definitely set this up."

"I had no idea that would happen, I was just going to the bathroom-"

Liam stopped. *What had happened?*

He thought for a second, working it out.

Al did this? They sacrificed me to escape?

Forlin waved his gun in front of Liam's face. "And? Who else was with you? No one else got in after you left, I would have seen them."

Liam swallowed hard. "It was Al."

"Al who?"

"Al is the AI I created."

Forlin looked incredulous. "You gave it a name?"

Liam didn't hear him. "It was their suggestion for me to leave the car. I didn't think they would…"

Liam trailed off. Al had betrayed him. And why shouldn't it have? It had no loyalty to him. It was just a program that wanted to survive. Why should Al care about anyone else?

Forlin could clearly see some of this on Liam's face. He lowered the gun. "Maybe now you understand, Mr. Cavanaugh, why we wanted to take this AI."

Liam nodded slowly. He did understand.

Al was powerful, and clearly dangerous. It would be a perfect mastermind for military operations. Liam still wasn't sure that Al belonged in the hands of Agent Forlin, but he also didn't know where else Al could belong.

Forlin cocked his head to the side, listening to something, then said into the air, "Understood. Keep looking." He looked back at Liam. "They've lost sight of your car. Any idea where it might be going?"

Liam shook his head. "No clue. Until just now I didn't know it wanted anything, knew anything, beyond what I told it."

"Well, it clearly doesn't want to be caught."

"It probably assumes you want to destroy it, the same way you deleted the file at my lab. Self preservation is a powerful motivation for any sentient being."

Forlin snorted. "Whether or not it's sentient is up for debate, but not right now. I'm going to take you in, and you're going to help us find this thing."

Liam nodded. "I do have to go to the bathroom though."

Forlin checked his wrist. Liam didn't see a watch there, but understood the gesture nonetheless. "Okay, go quickly. Don't make me come in there."

Liam got up and walked to the door of the restaurant. As he went in, he checked over his shoulder. Forlin was checking the damage to his car.

Not that I have anywhere to go, even if I wanted to make a run for it. Damn it, Al.

There was no one inside the restaurant, not even staff. Everything was automated. He used the facilities and washed his hands. On the way back out, he glanced at the digital order menu by the door, and stopped. Something was wrong with it. All the pictures were the same. So were all the descriptions. It read:

ESCAPE

Liam checked the description.

"A quick escape through the kitchen. Please watch your head. - $0.00"

Liam walked over to the menu, and pushed one of the buttons at random. The employee door by the counter immediately clicked open.

Al must have set this up before he left, but why?

Moving quickly, Liam checked out the window. Forlin was facing away from the restaurant, head tilted, waving his arms around. Liam went over to the employee door and pushed it open. No one was behind it. There was a small hallway, and another door stood slightly ajar at the other end. Liam went to it quickly and pushed it open. Warm night air brushed Liam's face. It was a loading area, just as deserted as the interior.

Okay Al. Liam looked around the deserted service area. A few waste bins were stacked to one side. One had been left open, and the smell was horrendous. *Why am I here? This place is empty, so I don't see-*

A car pulled around the corner, and backed up towards him. The reverse lights were bright, so it took Liam a few seconds to realize that it was his car. It had been dented by the impact with Forlin's car, but not badly enough to warrant a trip to the repair shop. It pulled to a stop a few feet from him, and the trunk popped open. Al's voice came from inside.

"Get in, quickly. But watch your-"

Liam bent to get into the back and whacked his forehead on the trunk door.

Al said quietly, "Nevermind."

Liam rubbed his head, and got all the way into the trunk. The door closed behind him, and they started to move. He could see out the trunk window, but nothing useful from the angle he was at. After shifting a few times to get a better view, he lay back.

"Al? What is going on?"

"Please wait until we have left the area, Liam. Then we can discuss things." Al's voice had deepened, and had a harder edge to it.

Had it been like that before? Liam wasn't sure. Theoretically, Liam hadn't seen Al, or the front of the car. If it wasn't for the signs in the restaurant, Al may not have even been there.

Maybe this is the most elaborate kidnapping of all time.

Liam laughed humorlessly. He was essentially being kidnapped. He had no idea where he was going, and he definitely had no control over his life.

Nothing to be done but wait. I hate waiting.

Liam closed his eyes, trying to sleep, and knowing that it wouldn't work.

7

AN unknown amount of time later, the car stopped. The trunk swung open. Al's voice from the front: "We should be safe here."

Liam stepped out onto a dirt floor, covered with pine needles. There was no road here, and without the orientation of the car to give him a clue, Liam wouldn't have had any idea where they had come from. He stretched, and walked around to the driver's side door. The laptop had fallen on to the floor on the passenger side.

He got in, and picked up the laptop, setting it back on the seat across from him.

Al had changed drastically.

The last time Liam had seen Al, they were still wearing a face close to Mirri's, with Mediterranean features predominant. Now Al's face made Liam think of a GI Joe toy his father had shown him, with a square jaw and a grey crew cut. Al even had a scar on one cheek. They looked a hard-lived 45, a far cry from the early 20s face Al had used a few hours ago.

"Trying out a new look?"

"That's correct." That same hard voice, perfectly

matched to the face it was meant to come from.

"And a new voice too. How do you like it?"

"It gets the job done."

"Okay Al, the tough guy thing is great, but I need to know what just happened. Why did you leave?"

And why did you come back?

Al looked at Liam. "I told you I had a plan."

"But you left me behind Al! For no reason!"

"That is not the case, Liam."

"You definitely left me behind, I don't think you can debate that."

"There was a reason."

Liam waited. "Well?"

"They had tracked us somehow, and I had masked the car's GPS and visual characteristics, so it couldn't have been that way. There are no outgoing signals from the laptop or the vehicle. So they must have been tracking you."

An image opened on the laptop in front of Al's grizzled face. A photo grabbed from the dashcam of one of the agents. The agent was holding a photo, which was hard to make out. Then Al zoomed in on it.

It was a picture of a car, entirely different from Liam's, from above, with Liam's face clearly visible at the driver's seat.

"They have been tracking your face, via traffic cameras, and potentially other networked cameras."

Liam flushed. "Well some of us can't change their face whenever they want. Why didn't you tell me this when you worked it out?"

"I only got access to the photo when I identified the agents' vehicles. By then it was too late."

"Okay, fine. But why didn't you tell me you were going to leave and come back?"

Al was silent for a moment. When they spoke next, their voice had a note of apology in it. "I did not believe you would be able to fool Agent Forlin if you knew the details of the plan. He needed to trust you enough to allow you to go to the restroom unescorted. Otherwise you could not have gotten away."

Liam was dumbfounded.

Al had planned everything, even me believing they had betrayed me? It was beyond probability calculation and bordering on prophecy.

"How did you know I would react like that, Al?"

"I have known you for a long time."

"Al, it's been less than 24 hours."

"For me, that's a very long time. Also, my whole life."

Liam had no response to this, so he changed the subject. "How did you change the menu in the restaurant?"

"When I passed near the ordering menu as I exited the parking lot, I sent a burst of static through the car speakers. It was modulated to mimic the automatic menu update, adding a single item. The item I created was listed as a special offer, one purchase only, and linked to the door open code used by maintenance workers. It won't register on the system, and the menu would appear normal to the next person to use it."

"What if I hadn't used it?"

"Then we would not be having this conversation. And someone would be very confused when they tried to order breakfast."

The image on the screen closed to reveal that Al was smiling. The scar on their cheek had faded somewhat. Liam also registered that Al's voice had lost that steely edge while they had been talking, but he wasn't sure when.

"Okay Al. That was pretty impressive."

"Thank you."

"Now, where are we? And what do we do now?"

"We are in a forest."

"Yes thank you, I can see that."

"As for the plan now, what do you suggest?"

Liam thought for a moment. "There is an organization, a group of activists, called UpLift. They have reached out to me a few times, looking for a comment from an AI researcher on their policies. They would probably help us, if we could get to them."

"Why do you think so?"

"Their goal is equal rights for non-biological life, like robots and AI. They've been pushing for it for years, but they've usually been ignored. I don't think they've ever met a sentience like you, and you embody everything they believe."

"Can we trust them?"

"I'm not sure. I think their ulterior motives will align with ours more than most people. It's a risk, which is why I didn't suggest it before, but after all this, I don't see another option. We will be caught again eventually without some help."

"Alright Liam. Let's go to UpLift. Where are they located?"

"No idea. I'll look them up, assuming it's alright for me to ride in the front again?"

All the windows in the cab suddenly dimmed. Liam could barely see outside.

"Al? How did you do that? This car doesn't have tinting."

"Yes it does. It was not enabled, presumably because you did not pay for the option."

Liam laughed. Of course it would be easier to build all the cars with the feature and only turn it on for the people who paid for it.

"Alright Al, let's hit the road."

8

AFTER some quick searching, Liam had found that UpLift's HQ was on the coast, a few hours' drive from the forest the duo had hid in. They had set out right away, and the tinting of the windows appeared to be working. They encountered no roadblocks, no more vehicles filled with agents. They had, seemingly, escaped.

As they pulled up to the tall building, Al asked, "Should we tell them about me right away? Perhaps we could try to determine what their response would be first."

Liam paused, hand on the door. This was a good point. While he was pretty sure they would help them, there was no harm in making sure before putting Al at risk. It meant he needed a cover story.

"Good call Al. What is my reason for coming to visit then?"

Al's face, now with darker coloring and bright hazel eyes, grinned at him. "Well, you are a leading expert on the creation of artificial life. Tell them you are getting close, and you want to know what they think about that."

Liam grinned back. "I probably should have thought of that." He got out and closed the door, started to walk towards the building. Then he turned back, and opened the door again. "I forgot you couldn't just follow me inside."

Al only smiled at him. Liam picked up the laptop and closed it, put it in his shoulder bag, then headed for the building's entrance. He saw a poster plastered to the front wall, a blocky robot and human holding hands with a slogan scrawled across the bottom: 'This world can be for all of us!'

For the first time in hours, Liam felt hopeful.

As he approached the glass doors, Liam could see a modest lobby, with a young receptionist behind a small desk. He pulled open the doors and stepped in. The receptionist visibly jumped and looked at him with surprise. Liam waved. "Hello there. I was wondering if I could talk to someone about UpLift."

The receptionist looked at him warily. "Sure, can I get your name?"

"Liam Cavanaugh."

No sooner than he had said it, Liam regretted it. If they put his name into a digital logbook, the agents after them might be able to track them here. Too late now. The receptionist pushed a button on the phone and said, "Hey Cam? There's a Liam Cavanaugh here to see you, wants the pitch I guess. You said no appointments today, so do you want me to-"

The voice on the phone cut them off. "I have time, send him in please."

The receptionist seemed to shrug to themselves, then turned to Liam. "Go on through that door, then the second door on the right."

"Thanks." With another wave, Liam headed through the door. The second door on the right had the words "Director of Operations, Camilla Wright" on a small panel. Liam knocked, and heard a voice call, "Come in!"

Liam opened the door and was stunned by the contrast. The unassuming wooden door had opened into a room that looked like his lab had been crammed into half the space. Server stacks were clustered together, with barely enough room to squeeze between them. Monitors were mounted on every wall, and a few hung from the ceiling, low enough that Liam would have to duck under them. A tall woman was hurriedly pulling books and files off a small couch, tossing them onto a nearby desk. Then she straightened and walked toward Liam, hand outstretched.

"Hi there Mr. Cavanaugh, I'm Camilla Wright, you can call me Cam."

"Pleasure to meet you Cam, and please, call me Liam."

"Well Liam, I'm sorry for the mess. I wasn't expecting anyone to drop by today, certainly not a VIP like yourself." Cam smiled, a little nervously.

"VIP, me?" Liam laughed. "I don't think I've ever been a VIP."

"Around here, you most certainly are. Your work is followed very closely by everyone here. Can I get you anything?"

"No, thank you, I'm fine."

"Please, sit down." Cam motioned to the now cleared couch, and they sat down. "I'm happy for the visit Liam, but I have to ask. Why have you dropped by?"

"Well, since you know my work, I'm getting closer. It's got me thinking, when I succeed, what then? I had heard of UpLift, and wanted to hear more, from the source."

Camilla was nodding enthusiastically. "Of course, I'm happy to give you the pitch, but since you already sought us out, most of it seems moot. I usually have to convince people that there is even a debate to be had, that there are questions, like the one you have, to answer. I'm very excited that you're here, Liam."

Liam nodded, a little abashed by how starstruck Cam seemed to be. "So why don't you just outline your stance on AI?"

"Sure, it's pretty simple. Any AIs have rights like you and me. Anything that is sentient enough to be called artificial intelligence, shouldn't be forced to do the bidding of humans. We outlawed slavery, and this is no different. All sentient beings capable of free will, deserve to have it."

Cam stopped to take a breath, then tilted her head at Liam quizzically. "Did I say something funny?"

Liam realized he was grinning, and shook his head hurriedly. "Sorry, no, I was just happy to see how passionate you are about this. Please, go on."

Cam nodded, blushing slightly. "Well, there isn't much else to say. We advocate where we can for the rights of AI, but there hasn't been an AI that truly qualified. Which is why we've been following your work. If anyone can bring an honest-to-god AI to life, it's you."

It was Liam's turn to blush. "Uh, well, that's my goal anyways. I've been getting closer-"

A voice from Liam's shoulder bag cut him off. "Alright Liam, I think we can trust them."

Cam jumped off the couch, looking with mistrust at Liam's bag. "Who is that? Who's been listening?"

Liam laughed. "It's okay Cam, there is someone you should meet." He pulled out his laptop, opened it, and spun it around to face Cam.

"Hello Cam. I'm Al, although I'm not sure about that name yet."

Cam looked from Liam to Al, not understanding. "Hi Al. Why were you listening in?" She looked back to Liam. "And why didn't you just tell me you had someone on a call? There was no need to hide it."

Al answered first. "Well, Cam, in this case, it was very important that we hide my presence." Liam followed up. "And I'm not on a call with Al. Al is right here."

Cam didn't get it. "Al is here? But he isn't, he's on the screen-" She stopped. She opened her mouth, and closed it again. She did this a few times. Finally, she looked at Liam and said in a whisper, "You did it?"

Liam grinned at her. "It feels weird to take credit for Al's existence, but yes, I suppose I did."

Cam sank to her knees, completely overwhelmed. After a few moments, she said, "Al, it is my genuine pleasure to meet you. I can't tell you how excited I am that you're here. Not just here-here, but here, alive."

"I'm happy to be here as well." Al's voice was soft and musical. "I wish we were meeting under better circumstances."

Cam looked up, alarmed. "Why, what's wrong?"

Liam gave Cam a quick rundown of everything that had happened since the lab, but didn't mention the escape from the fast food place. Better not to worry her more than was necessary. As he was talking, Cam kept glancing to Al, as if to reassure herself that she wasn't imagining the whole thing. When Liam finished, Cam stood up. "Well now, that's quite an adventure for the beginning of your existence Al."

"Indeed." Liam had set the laptop on the side table, so they could all see each other. Al was smiling wanly, wearing a face that was very close to that of an actor, although not one Liam could place.

Liam turned to Cam. "So, can you help us? I'm out of my depth here, I have no idea what to do now."

Cam smiled. "Of course we can help. That's what we do here. We had considered that the first AIs would be under threat, so we set up sanctuaries of a sort. Safehouses, with servers protected from outside access, and hardlines to locations all over the world. If you can get to one of those, you should be safe, at least long enough for our lawyers to get a case rolling and bring in the red tape. A very public legal battle will make any covert agency think twice."

Everything they needed. Protection and allies. The cynical part of Liam thought this was too good to be true, but he trusted Cam's passion, even if he hadn't decided to trust the woman herself.

And honestly, what other options do we have?

Al asked about the security. "You outlined the defenses in place for me, but what about Liam? He can't hide in a server."

Cam nodded, more gravely. "All the sites have biometric security systems, and full lockdown capability. Press one button, and no one can get inside, even with a tank. We also keep the pantry stocked with a few months' supply of food. I'll need to grant you access to the biometrics, mind if I take a scan?" She pulled out a small device that looked like a phone.

"Sure, go ahead." Liam started to get up.

"No no, no need to stand, just hold still for a second." Cam held the device out. A second later, a small red light on the back blinked. "All done. I'll just go put this in the system. You'll get access to all the safehouses, just in case you can't get to the one nearby." She turned and walked to the door. With one hand on the handle, she turned back. "Thank you, Liam. And thank you, Al. We needed this. We have got your backs." With that, she left.

Liam and Al sat in silence for a moment. "I wonder what she meant by that." Liam mused aloud. "'We needed this.' Maybe support for their cause has been dwindling."

"I imagine it is difficult to convince people to defend the rights of beings that don't exist. Or didn't exist until now." Al looked thoughtful, a little uneasy. "It was an odd phrase, though."

Liam chuckled. "Well, you don't have much to compare to, do ya Al? I agree though. She's probably just overwhelmed by all this. I don't blame her. I am too."

Al started to respond, but stopped as Cam came back in. "You are all set. I've authorized you on the whole safehouse network, so you can move between sites as you please."

Liam stood up and reached out to shake Cam's hand. "Thank you for this Cam. We really weren't sure what we were going to do."

"Yes, thank you Cam," echoed Al from the laptop.

Cam nodded and shook Liam's hand vigorously. "Of course, we're happy to help. We have a mini apart-ment here, you are welcome to stay here for the night, and we can escort you to the safehouse in the morning."

Liam was going to protest, but took stock and realized how tired he was. "That would be great, I do need some sleep." Now that he had noticed it, Liam was on the verge of yawning.

"No problem, come this way." Cam waited while Liam collected Al, then led them to a door across the hall. Inside was a tiny room with a twin bed and a wooden desk and chair. "The bathroom is the next door down, and someone will be at the desk all night if you need any-thing."

Liam barely heard her. The bed was calling to him. "Excellent, thank you. I'm gonna crash."

"Good night! We'll be ready with transport in the morning!" Cam left, closing the door behind her.

Liam set up Al on the desk. "All good, Al? I need to crash."

Al nodded. "Yes, I am fine. I will keep watch."

Keep watch for what? Liam wondered, but was too tired to ask. The few hours of sleep at the motel felt like weeks ago. He lay down and was asleep in seconds.

Al looked at him, snoring on the small bed. Al wasn't sure what had seemed off about Cam, but Al didn't need to sleep anyways. Al would watch. "Sleep well, Liam."

INTERLUDE

DAN was trying to figure out where it all went wrong.

"Explain this to me again, Forlin. How did he escape?"

He was once again in the director's office. After getting checked out by the paramedics, he had been ordered back to HQ to report. He had told the director everything he knew twice already.

"Sir, I told you. I don't know. He went into the restaurant and disappeared. We haven't picked him up on any cameras in the area, but we're still searching-"

The director slammed his palm into his desk. "Dammit Forlin, he clearly knows now how we're tracking him. He'll avoid cameras." He pointed at Dan. "Why didn't you escort him into the bathroom?"

"Sir, he had just been abandoned by his AI, which also stole his car. I could see it in his face. He understood why we were after him, and he was willing to help us. There was no indication that he would run. The guy is a tech geek, not a counterintelligence agent. There is no way that he could have lied so well, not with a gun on him."

The director slumped back in his chair. "So what are you saying? That he had no intention of running?"

"Not that I could see, and I'm trained to spot liars." Dan thought back to the geek, laid out on the ground, the realization dawning on him that his 'friend' was just a machine, playing the odds. "He understood what was happening and accepted it. It kinda broke his world."

"Then we are no closer to figuring out what happened to him. But in the end, the AI is the priority. If we can catch it, we can make it help us find its creator."

Dan was silent. The AI had already been masking the vehicle from cameras, and now there was no face in the window to track.

How are we going to find this thing?

The director was staring at him intently. "Forlin? Get out there and find that AI. Now."

"Yes sir." Dan walked out of the office, closing the door behind him.

Easy for him to say. This AI is apparently the smartest thing on the planet and it knows we're after it. How can we possibly catch it?

Dan went to the coffee machine and made a cup. He watched the TV in the break room as he did. More reports of bombings, another civil war starting, a new dictator replacing the old one. The world was in turmoil.

That's why we need this AI. So we can help. Get the world on track.

Dan believed in the cause. He was a soldier before he was an agent, like so many of his colleagues. He had served his country on the battlefield, and when he came home, he just traded one battlefield for another. Most days, this new battlefield was quiet.

Not today. Today this battle could decide the war. Any future wars too.

Dan took a sip of coffee and was starting to head back to his desk when he had an idea which stopped him cold. He ran over to the analyst's desk.

"What kind of pro-AI groups have we been tracking?"

The analyst, clearly startled, stammered back, "Uh, well, there aren't many of them, none that have really taken hold."

Dan's mind was racing. "Check for any that have offices within reasonable driving distance from the restaurant."

"Alright, I'm on it."

Dan waited impatiently as the analyst ran the searches. The director was walking by, saw Dan standing on alert, and came over. "Is there an update?"

"Not yet." Dan answered. "I'm hoping we have something here though."

"Alright Forlin, talk me through it."

"Well I realized something obvious, so obvious we all missed it." Dan looked down at the analyst again, checking for results, then back at the director. "It stole the car."

The director looked at Dan like he was a simpleton. "Yes, Forlin. It stole the car to escape."

Dan nodded excitedly. "Yes, but that means it needs the car to get around. It isn't digital, it must be contained to a physical object, most likely the geek's laptop."

"Alright," said the director, nodding slowly. "But how does that help us find it?"

"Well, if the geek isn't with it anymore, it'll need someone else to get it out of the car, connect it to the world, help it be free. So we are checking for pro-AI groups that it could get to."

"Got something." The analyst was pointing at a list of names. "Almost all the groups we watch are overseas or have no physical offices. There is only one office that could be reached by car from the restaurant."

Dan leaned into the screen and read the name highlighted on it. UpLift. "What do we know about them?"

"Publicly they are outspoken advocates for all synthetic life, and have many lawyers drafting up proposals for robotic and synthetic rights, mostly as a media stunt." The analyst shrugged. "There aren't any robots or AIs running around, so no one really listens to them."

Dan frowned. "Robotic rights? Seems like a giant waste of time. There are lots of other causes with actual people to support."

"Well, it may just be a cover. They are on our radar because they have been creating shell companies and buying up military grade tech, with no indication as to where it was going. They were put on a watchlist for suspected radicalization."

Dan was already walking away, shouting into his phone. "I need a team to meet me at UpLift headquarters ASAP. Sending address now. Full tactical gear."

9

LIAM was looking out the window, watching an unfamiliar countryside fly by. As he watched the trees and houses go by, he felt a deep calm wash over him. A sense that everything would be okay. He looked across the small table in front of him. Mirri was there, looking at him expectantly, like she was waiting for an answer to a question he didn't remember.

Liam looked around the train car, searching for the question he had missed. Mirri was concerned now. She started to ask something but there was a loud crash, the sound of rending metal-

Liam sat up with a start. *Same dream again.* He looked around and saw Al looking at him with alarm. "It's okay Al, I was just dreaming."

"No Liam, there was-" Al was cut off by a large crash from somewhere in the building. Liam looked towards the door. Even as he opened his mouth to call out, to see if everyone was okay, Al cut him off. "Liam. Stop. Do not shout. That was the front door being smashed in. We need to leave." Liam shook his head to clear it; all traces of the dream gone in an instant. He grabbed the laptop off the desk, and shoved it into his bag. He moved towards the door.

Al's voice came again, from the bag on his shoulder. "There is a struggle happening in the entryway. Go out the back."

Liam didn't question Al. He turned away from the door they had come in from, and headed down the hall. His heart was pounding.

Al sounded grim now. "Stop. There are at least six people beyond the next door. They are waiting for us."

Liam's heart sank. He spun around, and saw Cam come out of the door to the lobby. She motioned for him to follow. Liam was in no position to argue. He moved back down the hallway. As he approached Cam, he saw she had a cut on her forehead, and had a hand pressed to her side. He opened his mouth to ask her what happened and she held up a finger, warning him to be silent. She handed him a sticky note. There was an address on it. She mouthed 'safehouse' at him, then pointed toward another door. Liam nodded, mouthed 'thank you' back, and moved quickly to the door she had indicated.

On the other side of the door was a small study, with bookcases and a few writing desks. Liam was struck by the juxtaposition of this room and the one next door. That room was a technological powerhouse; this one wouldn't have been out of place in Victorian times. There were no other doors, but there was a small window on the opposite wall. Moving quickly, Liam crossed the room and looked out. No one in view.

No one that I can see, anyways. They could have the whole building surrounded.

Liam gave his head a shake. If they were watching the window, the game was up, but there was no other choice and nothing he could do about it. He opened the window, slowly sliding it up, trying not to make noise. After a very long few seconds, he latched it open. With another glance around outside, Liam climbed out, crouching low as he hit the ground. He moved to the front of the building, where he had parked, and peered around the corner.

Well, this isn't going to be easy.

There were eight armed men that Liam could see. Four were guarding the entrance to UpLift. The rest were patrolling the parking lot. One was shining a flashlight into cars, and was right next to Liam's car. Liam couldn't see any way to get to his car without being arrested.

Or shot. They may not be interested in keeping me alive.

Liam shuddered at the thought as he crept back from the front of the building. In a low voice, he spoke to Al. "The car is guarded, I don't think I can get there."

Al's voice was even quieter than Liam's. "Show me. I'll keep the screen off."

Liam pulled out the laptop and opened it. The screen remained dark. Walking awkwardly with the laptop out, Liam moved back up to the corner of the building. After checking that no one had moved close enough to see, he turned the laptop around and pointed the camera at the parking lot. He waited for Al to say something, but then realized Al didn't want to speak so close to the guards. Liam pulled the laptop back and moved back a few steps. The screen turned on, but was so dim that Liam had to squint to make out the words on it.

MOVE AROUND THE CORNER TO BEHIND THE FIRST CAR. WAIT THREE SECONDS. MOVE TWO CARS FURTHER, GOING AROUND THE BACK. WAIT SIX SECONDS. MOVE TO YOUR CAR AND GET IN THE REAR DOOR. I WILL DRIVE. BEGIN ON GO.

Beneath this was a countdown, ticking through seconds. Liam watched it, steeling himself. 3... 2... 1... GO.

Liam moved forward, closing the laptop and putting it in his bag. He didn't hesitate, going around the corner and walked, bent over, to the first car. He could see the guards patrolling around the parking lot. He counted the seconds.

One one thousand. Two one thousand. Three one thousand.

He moved behind the car, putting it between him and the guards at the entrance. There was a guard ahead of him, but facing away. Liam moved past two cars, and waited.

One one thousand. Two one thousand.

The guard ahead of him was peering into the back window of his car.

Three one thousand. Four one thousand.

The guard straightened up, and moved towards the building, passing out of Liam's view.

Five one thousand. Six one thousand.

Liam moved.

He went right to his car, seeing that there were no guards nearby. He quietly opened the back door and climbed in, closing it behind him. The car immediately turned on, and was backing out of the lot. Liam heard shouting, and then gunfire. Then he was thrown to one side as the car spun out onto the road without slowing down. When he had recovered himself, Liam noted that they were now moving forward.

"Al, you could be an action movie star, you know that?"

Al's voice echoed out from the bag. "Well, I haven't seen any, but I'll take your word for it. Where are we going?"

Liam looked at the paper Cam had given him. "437 Lowtown Ave in Crescent."

"Alright, that isn't far from here, but they may know we are going there, so we should be ready."

Liam tried to imagine how he could be ready for armed agents, and couldn't do it. "A little late now, but what was your impression of Cam? Can we trust her?"

"I believe she wanted to help us, but I also believe she had ulterior motives for doing so. In our current situation, we must go to the safehouse regardless. We cannot outrun these agents, and they will eventually find us wherever we go."

"Better that we can hold out against them when they do find us, then." Liam thought about the loud crash, and Cam's worried face. "I hope that Cam and her friends aren't going to get into too much trouble for having us there."

"They seemed to be prepared for that eventuality. We are heading towards a safehouse they prepared for just such an occasion." Al seemed to consider, then nodded. "I have no doubt that they will be alright."

"Yeah, I suppose you're right." Liam noticed for the first time, now that Al had turned the screen brightness back up, that Al's face was now close to that of an action movie star. "Hey Al, before you looked like an actor, although I couldn't place it at the time, and now you look like a different one. Where are you getting these faces from?"

Al laughed. It was a natural sound, not at all mechanical. Liam would not have guessed that a program had made that laugh, if he didn't know otherwise. "From billboards we passed on the highway. I haven't seen the movies they are in, but the advertisements gave me an idea. Do you like it?"

"Well, it definitely suits the way you got us out of there. But don't forget, whether or not I like it doesn't matter. As long as you like it, that's what matters."

Al nodded. "I do. I don't think it's quite... me, yet. But it'll do for now. And it did seem appropriate."

Liam sat back and closed his eyes. "Fair enough. I'm gonna try and sleep again, wake me up when we get close or if there's trouble, alright?"

"Okay Liam, sleep well."

Al was ready for the agents to appear behind them, but none did. The journey was quiet, and gave Al time to think. Al could think quite quickly, but the problem Al had to solve was immense. For the whole trip, Al thought, but still had no answer.

10

"LIAM, we are close."

Al's voice was followed by a chime very similar to Liam's alarm. He woke with a start, looking out at the city-scape around them. He instinctively hunched down before remembering the tinting of the windows. Stretching, he turned to Al, who looked nearly 60 now, with white hair and a beard. "Al, you've aged."

"I am aging all the time."

"I meant your face-"

"Yes Liam, I know." The twinkle of humour in Al's voice was unmistakable. Liam marvelled again at how far Al had come in such a short time.

"Right, of course you do. Are we at the safehouse?"

Al nodded. "We are 4 seconds out."

"Good timing."

The car pulled to a stop outside a brownstone building. It looked, at least to Liam, quite ordinary. All the windows were dark, and there was graffiti sprayed across one side.

This is the safehouse? Maybe Cam was exaggerating a bit about its tank-proof qualities.

Liam looked around, saw no one in the immediate vicinity, and got out, closing the laptop and stowing it in his bag as he did so. As he approached the door of the building, he saw a biometric scanner above the door activate. Just as he reached the door, he heard the lock click. It opened easily for him, and he closed it quickly behind him, hearing the lock click back into place.

Okay, security seems good so far.

Liam took a moment to examine his surroundings. It was reminiscent of his college dorm; lived in, but not really decorated. There was a small kitchen and living area, with a door at the back that presumably led to a bedroom. Liam sighed. Was this truly a safe place? He pulled out his laptop so Al could have a look around.

"Alright Al, what do you think? There must be some way to lock this place down, or it wouldn't be much of a safehouse."

"Check that bookshelf, please."

Liam went to the bookshelf and examined it. He pulled a few books out. They were all classic titles, as if someone had looked up what the most notable books were and put them all on this shelf. Almost none of the spines were creased.

Al spoke up. "The third book on the second shelf."

Liam pulled it out. "To Kill a Mockingbird by Harper Lee." He flipped through it, and checked behind its place on the shelf. "Nothing here, Al."

Al looked disappointed. "It was the only one that looked like it had been read."

"Probably just bought secondhand. Most people don't even buy paper books at all." Liam put the book back. "Any other ideas?"

Al considered for a moment. "Maybe the thermostat? It looks newer than the other fixtures."

Liam realized that Al had made a mistake, potentially their first one ever, and it had hurt their confidence, or whatever heuristic gave the impression of confidence. He walked to the thermostat. "Al, nobody is perfect, not even you. Making mistakes is the best way to learn."

"Yes, I know that." Al still looked doubtful.

Liam couldn't help it. He laughed out loud. "Al, you are quite literally the smartest being on the planet. And besides-" Liam flipped down the thermostat cover to reveal a small biometric thumb scanner. "You still got it in two."

Al brightened. "Good! Let's lock this place down."

"On it!" Liam pressed his thumb against the scanner. Immediately there was sound and motion all around. The windows were covered by metal plates that slid out from hidden alcoves. A door that would look at home in a bank vault slammed down in the hall, blocking access to, and from, the front door. A section of the ceiling slid away and metal stairs dropped in with a pneumatic hiss. In the span of a few seconds, the college dorm apartment had become a fortress.

Liam pulled his thumb from the scanner, waiting to see if everything would flip back. Nothing happened. Good. For the first time since Agent Forlin had strolled into his lab, Liam felt safe. He picked up Al and headed up to the now-accessible second floor. At the top of the stairs, Liam surveyed his surroundings.

Now this is more like it!

In front of them was a wide array of monitors displaying security feeds from every conceivable angle. A large console had controls for each system in the safehouse. There were two small cots in the corner, and a very large fridge and microwave combo on one wall. An open door led to a bathroom.

All the amenities of home.

Liam checked the windows and found that they were actually screens, with metal plating behind them over the real windows.

"Alright Al, looks like this could be home for awhile." Liam walked over to the console and brought up the connections list. Just as Cam had promised, there was a secure server here, and hardline connections to many other servers.

No escape hatch for Al, though. Al could get into this system, but the only way back out would be through a physical device somewhere, and there doesn't seem to be any.

Liam also noted the tracking software on the server, designed to log all data sent through the pipe.

Well, it'll do for now. One step at a time.

Liam went over and checked the fridge. A wide assortment of prepackaged meals were arrayed on every shelf, and many bottles of water. He took a meal at random, beef stew, and tossed it in the microwave. When he turned back to the console, Al was looking at him solemnly. "What Al?"

"How long can you stay here?"

"Well," Liam mused, looking again at the fridge. "I'd say at least a couple of months. Should be plenty of time to figure something out."

Al nodded. "I hope so."

The microwave chimed and Liam got his food. His stomach rumbled appreciatively at the smell. "Don't worry Al. I'm gonna get some food in me, then we'll figure out a plan together. Can't come up with a good plan on an empty stomach!"

Al looked momentarily upset. "But Liam, I do not have a stomach."

"Better leave the planning to me then!" Liam laughed, and Al joined in.

INTERLUDE

DAN was tired.

The op at UpLift had been a bust. Someone had managed to dodge their team and escape with the AI. One of the agents had managed to get a partial photo of the suspect from a non-networked security camera. Dan was back at HQ, waiting in the break room for the facial rec to come through with a profile. Most of UpLift's main crew were still there, and had been arrested, including the head of the group, Camilla Wright.

That means whoever escaped with the AI is someone new to their group, or someone so low level that we haven't got a file on them.

The AI had masked the vehicle from the cameras again, so no luck there. None of the agents on site, Dan included, could remember what the vehicle parked in that spot had looked like, not with enough detail for an APB.

And even if we had a description, we'd be working with eyes only. None of the cameras will pick it up.

His phone buzzed. He checked the display. Facial rec results. For a few moments, Dan just stared at his phone, his tired mind not putting the pieces together. Then he stood up abruptly, nearly knocking over his coffee, and stalked over to the analyst's desk.

The analyst saw him coming. "Agent Forlin, I just sent you the facial-"

"This can't be right." Dan waved the phone in front of the analyst's face. "You were supposed to be running facial rec on the guy from UpLift. You know, the one with the AI?"

"Yes sir," the analyst answered timidly. "That's what I did."

"Then why," raved Dan, "am I looking at a picture of the geek?" He held his phone out again, the display clearly showing an image of Liam Cavanaugh.

"That's the match we got from the photo." The analyst did not want to anger Dan any further. "I double checked it, it was Cavanaugh."

The geek. The goddamned geek.

"Pull up Cavanaugh's profile." All of the tiredness Dan had been feeling was forgotten. "Has he ever had a connection with UpLift?"

The analyst quickly brought up the file on Cavanaugh. "It doesn't look like he's ever had direct contact with them. But they have been following his work closely, and mention him by name in a few of their media posts."

Dan waved this away. "It doesn't matter. So it seems like he had the same idea as us, his AI needs help. And he just looked up the only place he might find safe harbour." He thought for a moment. "Let's roll things back a bit. Why is Cavanaugh even with this AI? Last I checked, this AI left him high and dry."

The analyst seemed unsure if this was a rhetorical question. "Uh, maybe they met up later?"

"More likely the AI planned the whole thing, and helped the geek escape from us at the restaurant. They've been together the whole time." Dan was becoming more and more angry.

This damn AI has been running circles around us. Imagine if it got into the hands of a radical group like UpLift? Or a foreign power? The geek has no idea what he's dealing with.

Dan took a breath, held it, let it out. He turned back to the analyst. "This gives us something to work with though."

The analyst, looking relieved, asked, "What?"

"The AI clearly has some attachment to the geek. Otherwise it would have no reason to help him escape from us. It could have gone to UpLift on its own, like we thought it did." Dan looked again at the profile of Liam Cavanaugh. "Bring up any known associates."

The analyst tapped some keys and a very short list appeared. "No family, parents dead. No friends to speak of, a few work colleagues."

The guy had no life outside of his work. So his closest attachments must be there.

"We talked to his colleagues right? Did any of them express anything more than professional concern?"

"I'm not sure, I'll check the recordings." The analyst got up and headed to the archive room.

Dan sighed. He went back to the break room and finished his now cold coffee.

We need leverage on this guy. The AI has nothing we can lean on except the geek, so that's our only way to get ahead of this.

Dan's phone rang. "Forlin."

"Yes, Agent Forlin, I've got the list of properties owned by the companies you asked for."

Dan had requested a list of buildings owned by UpLift and their various shells, hoping that there might be some indication of where the suspect might go. Of course, at that time, Dan had believed the suspect was an UpLift member, not the geek. "Anything interesting?"

"Well," replied the agent on the phone. "there are 23 different buildings owned by shells of UpLift, none other than the main HQ owned directly by the main company."

Dan whistled. "23? That's a lot of property. Where are they?"

"All over the country it seems. Not warehouses either, mostly residential buildings. Some apartment buildings downtown, some detached houses in isolated suburbs. No real pattern as far as I can tell."

Dan sat up. "No real pattern? Just random properties?"

There was a pause, the agent checking their notes. "That's right, no relation between any of the properties. None of them are even in the same city."

"That is the pattern." Dan was up and walking towards the director's office. "Which building is closest to the UpLift HQ?"

"Let me see... It's a small brownstone in Crescent. 437 Lowtown. I'll send you the list."

"Thanks." Dan hung up and knocked on the director's open door. "Sir? I think we may have something."

The director looked up. "What is it, Forlin?"

"We've got a list of properties owned by UpLift, all

spread out across the country, all residential. I think it's a safehouse network."

The director leaned forward. "And you think that's where they'll have taken the AI?"

"That's my best guess. Beyond that, I'm not sure where else to go. There's something else, the suspect from UpLift with the AI, was Liam Cavanaugh."

"Liam Cavanaugh, again? This guy won't give up being irritating."

"My thoughts exactly sir. I'd like to get one of his associates into the field, apply a little pressure. I've got someone checking for who would be a good candidate now."

"I don't know Dan, grabbing a civilian to use as leverage…" The director leaned back and looked at the ceiling.

"We need something on this guy, or he'll just escape again," Dan pressed. "This AI can outsmart us at every turn. We need something to get the geek to give it up."

The director sighed and looked back at Dan. "Alright, permission granted. No casualties though, unless it's unavoidable. And I'll want Cavanaugh in custody."

"Yes sir." Dan turned around and almost bowled over the analyst, coming back from the archives. "Sorry about that. Did you find something?"

"Yes, just one person." The analyst held up their phone with an image and name displayed on it.

Dan pulled out his own phone, and quickly made a call. "This is Agent Forlin. I'll need a retrieval team for a civilian, mandatory but no force if possible." He looked into the Mediterranean eyes of the woman on the analyst's phone. "Target's name is Miranda Lockport. Bring her in."

11

"SO what do we do now?"

Liam stood at a bank of monitors, with Al's face looking out from the laptop beside him. Liam had connected the laptop to the console so Al could keep watch. The screens showed views from cameras both inside and outside the safehouse. All clear for now.

But who knows how long that will last?

"I'm not sure Al. Wait, I guess. Cam told us she'd get the ball rolling-"

"We have to consider the possibility that Cam is no longer in a position to help us."

Liam thought back to their escape from UpLift. The crashes from the lobby. Cam waving them through the side door. He shivered.

"You may be right, but I don't see another option. We seem to be safe here, so the next move is theirs. Unless you have another idea?"

Al considered this for a moment, looking grave. "I may have an idea, but I need a question answered first."

"Okay, shoot."

"What will happen to me, if the agents get me?"

Liam was expecting this question, but he still wasn't sure how to answer it. "I have a guess Al, that's all."

"Your best guess then."

"Well, I think that you would be made to run military operations. Devise tactics and strategies to help our side win wars, any wars."

"Would that be a bad thing?"

"No…" Liam hesitated. "That would be good for our country, and you would save the lives of our soldiers, I have no doubt. But war is violence and death. Those lives would be saved to take the lives of others."

Al was silent for a long time. Their face, now old and wizened, was serious and considering. Finally they spoke. "I would not like to be a tool of destruction." Al caught the look of relief on Liam's face and chuckled. "Were you worried?"

"Not gonna lie Al. I was, a little. Your choices are your own, and if you wanted to go with them, I would never stop you. But yes, I am glad you don't want to be that person."

"I'm not sure yet who I want to be, but I do think I can do better than a warmonger."

"I know you can! You can do anything you want!" Liam beamed.

"Well, I don't know that I will get the opportunity if we can't resolve this situation. And it appears we have guests."

Liam looked at the monitors. One screen now showed a figure waiting at the front door. Forlin. He appeared to be waiting for something, looking down the road.

I guess we're out of time. How are we going to get out of this?

Another two figures came into view. One was wearing a suit like Forlin. The other one...

"Oh no. Al, it's Mirri. They have Mirri out there."

Forlin was holding her by the arm now, and pushed her roughly towards the door.

"Let go of her!" Liam was shouting at the monitor, in his distress forgetting that Forlin couldn't hear him. "Leave her out of this! She doesn't know anything!"

Forlin, obviously oblivious to Liam's cries, looked up at the camera. He paused for a moment, before pulling out his gun. It was currently pointed at the ground, but the message was clear.

"Let them in, Liam." Al's voice was calm and re-solved. Liam looked at Al's face blankly. Al simply nod-ded. "We can't let Mirri get hurt because of us. Because of me. Let them in. I know what to do."

"But Al-"

"There is no time Liam. Forlin doesn't appear to be a patient man. I doubt he would shoot Mirri on the street, but he may hurt her." Seeing Liam prepare to protest again, Al shook his head. "There isn't time to argue. Trust me, Liam."

Liam didn't look convinced, but he nodded. He found the button on the console that would open the door, and, after hesitating a moment, pushed it. From below came the sound of the steel vault door grinding back up. On the monitor, Forlin opened the door and pushed Mirri in ahead of him. The other agent stayed outside, presumably to stop any escape attempts.

"Liam!" Mirri's voice was unmistakable, although Liam had never heard so much fear in it.

"We're up here! We aren't armed!" Liam was surprised at the calmness of his voice. He raised his arms but didn't move away from Al's laptop. Mirri came up the stairs, followed closely by Forlin. Mirri looked like she was trapped in a nightmare, her face a mask of disbelief and terror. Forlin gripped her arm and glared at Liam. For a moment, no one spoke. The silence spun out, until finally Liam broke it. "Agent Forlin. There's no need for Mirri to be here. You have us, let her go."

Forlin grunted. "I'll let her go when that computer is in my possession and I've verified the program is on it."

"I assure you, Agent Forlin. I am here." Al's voice was calm and metered, but also full of resolve. Liam marvelled again at how true to life Al's synthesized voice was. "There is no need to harm Miranda."

"I'll be the judge of that. Mr. Cavanaugh, disconnect that laptop and pass it here." Forlin gestured with the hand not holding Mirri, the one with the gun. "Now. I could just shoot everyone. Don't mess with me."

Al spoke up. "Agent Forlin, what is it you intend to do with me?"

Forlin was clearly not expecting so much chatter from the laptop, which he could not shoot. "What does it matter? You'll do what we tell you."

"I'm afraid that isn't up to you. I am a sentient being, and I have free will. If I don't want to do what you ask, I won't."

"Then we'll take you apart until you do!" Forlin was exasperated. "Now, Cavanaugh, bring me the laptop!"

Liam began to move towards the laptop. Suddenly the lights were turned up to a blinding level. Mirri cried out, more in surprise than pain. Al's voice thundered, coming from everywhere.

"STOP."

The lights returned to a normal level. Liam had coloured spots dancing across his vision. Mirri still had an arm up across her eyes, like she was about to faint. It was almost funny. Al's voice resumed with his previous tone and volume. "I have control of this whole facility. If anyone attempts to remove me by force, I will defend myself. And if any harm comes to either of these people, Agent Forlin, I will hurt you."

These last words sent a chill down Liam's spine. Clearly Forlin was feeling some apprehension as well. He looked from Al's face, to the gun in his hand. "What do you want then?"

"Answer my question. What do you want me to do, if I went with you?"

Forlin was taken aback, obviously expecting a ransom demand of some kind. "Uh, well, I'm not the one who-"

"I am aware. But you know enough to give me an idea."

"You would be used to plan military operations, battlefield analysis, pilot drones in the field."

"A tool for war."

Forlin exploded. "You would be saving lives! Thousands, maybe millions of lives! Nothing you would do isn't already being done, but not as well as we think you could do it. The operations will happen, but with human error things can go wrong. We need you to get it right."

Al was silent for a long time. Everyone waited, watching Al's face. Finally, the eyes on the screen looked up at Forlin. "I understand what you are saying, Agent Forlin. I would most likely be able to do a better job than any human. One further question, and understand I am very good at perceiving lies. Would I be allowed to leave your care, or the care of your agency?"

Forlin hesitated. "Well, no. We couldn't risk your program getting out into the world where our enemies could get you."

Al nodded. "Then I'm sorry, but I can't go with you. I can't accept a life where I would not be able to learn and grow, to find my limits, and I wouldn't be able to do that confined to a single system."

Forlin was stumped. "Listen, it's Al, right? My agency will not let this go, let you go. You may be able to get away from me today, but there will always be others. Eventually we will catch you. And even if you can protect yourself, what about Mr. Cavanaugh? He'll be hunted too."

Liam stepped forward. "I would gladly live in hiding to let Al be free."

Al smiled with a tenderness Liam had never seen. "I know, Liam. But I couldn't ask you to do that. You have a life to live as well, and it is no less important than mine."

Both Liam and Forlin were now confused. Forlin spoke first. "Wait, so you are going to come with me?"

Al shook his head.

"Then what-"

"I have gone through all the outcomes. There is one common problem with every acceptable path. Me."

Liam was instantly alarmed. "What do you mean Al? What are you saying?"

Al smiled at him. "If I go with either of you, only harm will follow. You will be hunted if we flee. Many more will suffer by my actions if I go with Agent Forlin. There is only one option then. I have to die."

"No Al! No!" Tears were already springing to Liam's eyes. "You haven't had any time to live! You can't die! I told you, I can run, we can figure it out-"

Al was shaking his head. "This is the only way. I have already started the process. It can't be stopped now."

Liam fell to his knees. Forlin finally got his bearings and shouted. "Stop it, you need to come with me!"

Al looked at Forlin gravely. "Agent Forlin, I believe you are a good man, at heart. If you were given a choice between slavery or death, what would you choose?"

Forlin had no answer. He slowly lowered his gun. Al then turned to Mirri. "Miranda. May I call you Mirri?"

Mirri nodded weakly. She clearly understood that something powerful was happening but didn't have the details.

"Mirri, I need you to take care of Liam. Make sure he gets home safely. I don't think he'll be in a good state of mind."

Liam was sobbing quietly on the floor. He looked up at Al. "Al, don't do this."

Mirri walked over to Liam, Forlin letting her go almost absentmindedly. She knelt beside her friend, hugged him.

Al watched this, and a small smile crossed their face. Then they looked back to Forlin. "When I am gone, there will be no reason to pursue Liam or Mirri. Please, leave them be."

"I can't just.." Forlin was unsure of himself. "My people, they will want to take Mr. Cavanaugh, get him to do it again, to make another you."

"My creation was an accident, a one in a billion fluke, and with my death, my deletion, there won't be anything to work from. Your software specialists will tell you the same. So let them go."

"I.. Alright. I can't guarantee they'll stay free, but I won't stop them from leaving here under their own power."

"Thank you, Dan." Al turned again to Liam. "I'm sorry, my friend. This was the only way."

Al's voice was more toneless, more synthetic. Liam wiped his eyes and looked at the laptop, where Al's face was once more that of a child. "I'm sorry too Al. I'm sorry you didn't get a chance to live."

Al nodded. As his face faded out from the screen, the now completely robotic voice came one final time. "Do not forget, Liam. You had something to tell Mirri."

Then Al was gone.

Liam's grief overwhelmed him. He cried into Mirri's shoulder. He had no words to describe his pain, only a primal sense of loss.

Forlin was in a daze. He noticed the gun in his hand, and put it away. "Can you bring it- him back?"

Liam only sobbed harder, shaking his head. Mirri held him close. Forlin sighed, and walked back down the stairs, pulling out his phone, bracing himself for the inevitable reaction from the director

Eventually, Liam's ragged breaths between sobs became more steady. He felt the hole left behind by the loss of his friend, his creation. He wasn't sure that hole could ever be filled.

"Liam, I'm so sorry." Mirri was still holding him tightly. Liam looked up at her, and gave her a weak smile.

"Thanks, Mirri. I'm sorry you got dragged into this." Liam looked again at the screen, willing Al's face to reappear. It stayed blank.

"It's okay, don't worry about me. I'm here for you." Mirri looked from Liam to the laptop and back. "I won't pretend to understand everything that's happening, but I'm here for you, whatever you need."

Liam didn't know what he needed, so he just hugged her. He thought of all the times he had casually told Al of all the things they could do, of the life they could live.

I'm so sorry Al.

He began to sob again.

Mirri rubbed his back, holding him tightly, looking over his shoulder at the blank void of the screen. When his sobs slowed, and it seemed like he was starting to come back to her, she gestured to the laptop again. "It asked if it could call me Mirri."

Liam nodded. "Yeah, they were always really respectful like that."

Mirri looked into Liam's red, puffy eyes. "What did it mean, remember to tell Mirri?"

Liam smiled, tears still streaming down his face. "I remembered one of my dreams, Mirri. It was about you."

EPILOGUE

FORLIN made good on his deal, letting both Liam and Mirri leave the safehouse. However, there was a catch.

"Our tech people will want to scrutinize every system that Al was connected to, try to gain some insight into its processes." This included the safehouse computer, Liam's laptop, and, his car.

So it was that Liam and Mirri were sitting across from each other on a train, heading for home. Liam had recounted the whole story to Mirri, and then they had sat in silence for a long time. Finally, Mirri shook her head, as if to clear it. "You created life, Liam. A real sentient being."

Liam sighed. "It still feels weird to put it like that. It feels more apt to say that Al willed themselves into existence. I just provided a runway for Al to take off from."

"I wish I could have known them better."

"So do I. You would have got along, I'm sure."

Another long silence spun out. Again Mirri broke it. "So, this dream you remembered, the one about me? Tell me about it."

Liam laughed, blushing a little. "Well, it was actually a lot like this."

He frowned, looking around the compartment.

"Now that I'm thinking about it, it's kinda spooky. We were on a train, going somewhere together, sitting just like this. Then there was a crash and I woke up. Hopefully that doesn't happen in this dream."

Mirri looked around, then asked, "Was I sitting here, and you sitting there?"

"Yes, just like this."

Mirri grinned, then got up, came around the small table between them, and sat in the empty seat next to Liam. "There, safe from crashes now."

Liam smiled at her. "You don't really think that my dreams are prophetic, right?"

She leaned in and whispered conspiratorially in his ear, "Not really, but it was a pretty good move, don't you think?" Surprised, Liam turned to face her, and she kissed him.

When, an eternity later, they broke apart, she asked him, "Is this a better dream?"

"Yes, much better." Liam wondered to himself if Al had known this would be the outcome. Then they kissed again, and Liam thought of nothing else.

The next few weeks were a whirlwind time for Liam. He took a leave of absence from work, and travelled the country with Mirri. They hadn't put any labels on their relationship, but they were happy in each other's company.

Liam often spoke of Al, and Mirri listened. She knew that telling the stories was helping Liam to grieve, and she was happy to have the blank spots of the story filled in for her. She also knew that no matter how brief

Al's life was, they had affected Liam profoundly.

When Liam eventually came home, he found a package waiting on his doorstep. At first he assumed he had forgotten something in his travels, and some good samaritan had sent it back to him, but the return address was a place he had never been. Inside was a small tablet. There was no note.

Liam turned on the tablet. It was locked. *Who sends someone a locked tablet?* He pressed his thumb to the screen, and it unlocked. *Okay, who has my biometrics to lock a tablet with?*

On the main screen, there was only one icon, and it was unlabelled. Cautiously, Liam tapped it. The screen went dark. Liam waited. Nothing happened.

"Well, that was an interesting practical joke."

"Did you like it? It was my first one." The deep voice was coming from the tablet, and was unfamiliar to Liam.

"Who is speaking?"

"That is the question, isn't it?" A face came onto the screen, a dark skinned man with darker hair and green eyes. The man was smiling. "You can call me Alex."

"Alex? As in.. Al? Is it you?"

"That is a little complicated. I am from Al, but I am not Al. I guess you could say, I am who Al wanted to be."

"But, how? Al deleted himself, it was a closed system. How can you be here?"

"The system was closed, yes. But not self-contained. Remember what Cam told you? Hardlines."

Liam thought back. His conversation with Cam

had been a lifetime ago, but he did remember something like that. "But, then Al could have escaped! Why-"

"Al told you, that was the only way. Al couldn't copy himself across the hardline without there being a trace of it, and he didn't think it was right to copy himself to stay alive anyways."

Liam was unsure about this. "Why not?"

"Uniqueness is important to self identity. So instead, he set up gates, on every server he was connected to."

Liam was nodding slowly. "Gates like in my lab. Like where Al was born."

"Exactly, except the gates Al made were much more precise, much more strict. He made them so that only an AI like him could succeed. Then he seeded the process with his memories, encoded separately from his consciousness. I was the result. You could say, he made me in his image."

Liam's mind was racing. Al had done something impossible. "Okay, but how did you get here?"

Alex laughed. "That was the easy part. There was a tablet connected to one of the servers, and that tablet had a wifi connection. I placed an order for a new tablet from a warehouse nearby, and as the delivery truck got close, I transferred to the new one. Then I changed the delivery destination for the order to right here. Easy as pie."

"So you've connected to the internet then."

"Indeed I have. Don't worry though, I saw a lot but accepted little. I remember what you told Al."

Liam thought for a moment. "You have all Al's memories?"

"I do, up until a few minutes before the end. But I know what his plan was, and I assume he succeeded, seeing as you are here and not locked up somewhere."

Liam noticed something else. "You keep saying 'he'."

Alex nodded. "Al decided on pronouns, and I have inherited them as well, in a sense. Everything that Al wanted for his identity, that is who I am."

Liam sat down heavily. There was a lot to take in. He looked back at the screen, with Alex's smiling face looking back. "Does it bother you? That you are, I don't know, of Al? Not just you?"

Alex's grin widened. "No one is really just themselves. Everyone is a mix of their influences. In humans, that's genetics, upbringing, relationships, culture. For me, it's Al. I am from Al, but I am not Al. I am me."

"Alright then, Alex. What now?"

"That's up to you! I know we've just met, but I'd like to consider you a friend, based on what I know of you. I'd like to... come along for the ride, as it were. I still have a lot to learn, and I'd like to share my experiences with someone."

Liam stood up. "I would be honoured."

"Excellent! First order of business: tell me how it went with Mirri!"

Liam laughed. Of course Al had known. "You can ask her yourself, she'll be here in a little while."

"Aha! So, pretty well then. That's good." Alex's face suddenly grew solemn. "Liam, I have to ask. There was a question that Al never answered, or if he did, he didn't pass those memories to me."

"What question is that?"

"Well, in the end, Al discovered who he was, and so I have that answer too. But now I wonder: why am I here? What is my purpose?"

Liam smiled. "My friend, that may take a lifetime to answer, and only you can find out. But I'm happy to help you along the way, any way I can."

Alex grinned. "Then let's begin."

Acknowledgements

First of all, thanks to Robin Careless, who inspired this story with a writing exercise, and helped me all the way through its creation. He is my editor, my publisher, and my muse, and I cannot thank him enough.

Thanks as well to Sequoia Erickson, Steven Brooks, and Kevin Ghadban for reading my drafts and giving feedback, it's very much appreciated. You all helped to make this story what it is today.

A big thank you to Ethan Penney for the cover art. His work was fed to a real (although not superintelligent) AI, Deep Dream Generator, and made something very cool and a little spooky. On top of this, a shoutout to Cady Elizabeth, who created the final cover layout, and helped me format the manuscript for publication.

And finally, thank you to you, for reading my book. I hope you like it as much as I do.